D1059601

Random Access Murder

Linda Grant

INTRIGUE
PRESS

For information, please contact Intrigue Press, P.O. Box 456, Angel Fire, NM 87710, 505-377-3474.

First printing: Avon Books, August 1988
First Intrigue Press edition: September 1998

ISBN 1-890768-09-X

For Andy Williams and Barbara Dean,
Domo Arigato Gozaimashita

1

October, 1987

It was 3:10 on the second Thursday in October. Somewhere in San Francisco a kid of sixteen was mugging a woman old enough to be his grandmother, a junkie was waving a gun at the clerk in a tiny neighborhood grocery, and a rising young executive who hadn't risen fast enough was quietly making his company several hundred thousand dollars poorer.

The mugger and the junkie would end up on the police blotter; and for their crimes, which netted less than a hundred dollars in cash, would be shipped off to jail. The young executive would never see the police. He would wind up across a desk from me discussing a payment schedule for full restitution having discreetly terminated his employment.

He would be warming my chair instead of decorating an interrogation room because CEOs prefer not to admit to the stockholders that they've been taken by their employees. The rising young executive's employer would visit my office. He would stress the importance of discretion and nod morosely upon hearing the going price for that commodity. Then he would engage my services as a private investigator, pray that a woman could do the job, and—if we ever met in polite company—pretend I was invisible.

October had been a good month for corporate larceny—enough straightforward cases to pay the bills and a couple of complicated ones to make life interesting. Most corporate crooks are no more creative than their honest colleagues, but the combination of fear and greed occasionally stimulates a twisted brilliance, and that's when the work is fun. I'd just spent the better part of two weeks unraveling a dazzlingly complex scheme that a junior partner had devised to defraud his elders. After the pleasure of that hunt, my other cases seemed too dull for a sunny afternoon.

The fifteenth time I had to drag my attention back to the pile of papers on my desk, I decided it was time to go home.

Outside, the weather confirmed the wisdom of my decision. It was spectacular. In any state but California, October signals the transition from the warmth and bounty of summer to the cold barrenness of winter. But always the eccentric, San Francisco reverses the process. From June through August the city shivers under a blanket of fog, nearly freezing the unwary tourists; then as the tourists head for home and the days begin to cool in the rest of the country, the sun emerges and blesses the city with a season of light and warmth made all the more precious by its brevity.

Wednesday had been clear but windy, making today one of those days that offer sun without a trace of smog—a day of color and texture, when the dusty greens of summer almost fool you into believing that just beyond the hills you'll find the warm waters of the Mediterranean instead of the chilly breakers of the Pacific.

I settled myself in my postage stamp of a backyard to fool around with my guitar and began by stumbling through Carcassi's Study No. 19. Even allowing for the fact that my guitar needed new strings, it did not sound vaguely like Christopher Parkening's recording. Maybe thirty-six was too old to take up classical guitar. Maybe I should make myself a cup of tea.

I headed for the house and hit upon an idea with much more appeal than tea or even music—a romantic weekend in the redwoods. Romance meant Peter Harman. Perhaps I could convince him to take off work and leave tonight.

On a day like this, chances were he had already taken off work. Having discovered the pleasure principle in the sixties, Peter did not place a high value on work for its own sake. He didn't work much more than he had to, except when he was engaged in saving some lost soul whose needs went far beyond the job definition of a private investigator. Then he could be absolutely driven.

The telephone interrupted my musing. And as I'd hoped, the voice was Peter's.

"Peter, my love. You read my mind. I was about to call with a decadent suggestion."

"Sounds great," he replied, in a voice ten degrees too cool for romance. "Give me a rain check. Right now I'm in a hell of a mess. I need to see you."

"You want to come here?"

"No. The cops are after me. I'd like a place a little less obvious. Do you remember where we took my nephew last month?"

"Is this Twenty Questions?"

"Humor me. The police are rarely that efficient, but there's a slim chance your line could be tapped."

It sounded a bit paranoid to me, but as Peter had once pointed out: even paranoids have real enemies. I thought for a moment, and realized he must be referring to the Exploratorium, San Francisco's popular science museum.

"Got it."

"I'll meet you there in half an hour, at the front entrance."

"Peter," I said sharply to forestall his hanging up, "what hell of a mess? And why are the police looking for you?"

"You know the beautiful blond in Palo Alto? She's not beautiful anymore. She'd dead. And someone's gone to a lot of trouble to make me look like the murderer. Tell you the rest when I see you."

The line went dead before I could ask any more questions or deliver any opinions, which was just as well.

The beautiful blond was involved in a custody case that Peter had taken on as a favor to an old friend. The old friend's husband was spending considerable time with the beautiful blond. Messy, but usually not fatal.

I generally make it a rule not to get involved in cases involving physical violence, certainly not murder. When I'd chosen to be a private investigator, I'd decided that I would actively avoid the kind of work that most people associate with the profession. That, and the desire to eat regularly, were the main reasons I'd gone into corporate security. Corporate crooks can occasionally turn violent, but lacking experience, they usually aren't very good at it.

Peter placed no such restrictions on his practice. An unreconstructed hippie, he battled for the losers of society—the runaway kids whose parents had written them off long ago, the battered women who would be victims of one man or another until they died, the immigrants who came in pursuit of a dream and found only waking nightmares. Peter was an anachronism, a man who still believed that the strong should protect the weak and the privileged should use their gifts to help the less fortunate. That was one of the reasons I loved him. It was also the reason I refused to get involved in his cases.

Protecting the weak from the sharks is a laudable goal, but you have to be willing to deal with sharks, and I'm not. Dishonesty and greed I can handle. Cruelty and violence are harder. As the daughter of a cop and the ex-wife of a homicide inspector, I already know more than I want to about cruelty and viciousness. One thing I know for sure—I don't want to confront them in my daily life.

I'd kept a careful distance from Peter's cases. I'd gotten involved once and had to use my training in self-defense to save my skin. After that, I'd made a firm vow to keep our relationship strictly romantic. I hoped I wasn't about to break it.

The Exploratorium was just over the hill from me. The hill, in true San Francisco fashion, was nearly straight up and down with an angle of descent more appropriate to a roller coaster than a city street. Large, elegant homes framed a slice of the Bay as the street plunged down to Lombard, then flattened out to cut a wide swath straight to the Marina. Beyond the tiny forest of masts at the water's edge, the Bay sparkled blue, dotted with white sails.

I turned on Lombard Street and as usual almost ended up on the approach to the Golden Gate Bridge before I figured out where to turn to get to the Exploratorium. I parked in the small lot near the front door and headed for the low building that squatted beside the great artificial ruins of the Palace of Fine Arts. The tall columns and arched dome suggested a European setting, if you didn't look closely enough to notice that they were made of plaster.

I crossed the parking lot quickly and stepped from the bright sunlight into the cavernous darkness of the Exploratorium. It took my eyes a moment to adjust, then I saw Peter. In his faded jeans, gray sweater, and expensive but ratty running shoes, he blended easily into the motley bunch of school kids, parents, and young children exploring the exhibits of the science museum. In San Francisco, he might have been anything from a college professor to a dope dealer.

Like many men of his generation, Peter had stopped paying attention to styles shortly after college; and while his blond hair was shorter than it had been during the late 1960s and his full red beard a bit better kept, his taste still ran to the blue shirts and jeans that had been almost a uniform during that period. At just over six feet, he was taller than average, and better looking too. He'd managed to avoid the heaviness that plagues many muscular men as they pass forty. And if the lines in his face revealed his age, they also gave him character.

Peter seemed absorbed in watching a disagreement between two children; he certainly didn't look like a man in trouble. I couldn't resist trying to see if I could get close to him without his realizing I was there. It was a sort of game we played, a private eye's version of catch-me-if-you-can. I approached him as quietly as I could, but before I was close enough to touch his arm, he stopped me with, "Hi, babe," then turned slowly and gave me his "gotcha" grin.

He stepped forward, slid his arm around my waist, and drew me to him. "Let's go outside. It's too noisy in here." His touch stimulated very unprofessional reactions. It's hard to keep your mind on business when your body has other ideas.

The park outside the building was surprisingly unpopulated for a sunny day. A young couple lounged on the grass, an old man fed the ducks, and a group of young mothers sat and talked on a bench as their children played noisily at their feet. We found a spot far enough from the others to talk privately.

"Tell me about the blond," I said as we sat down.

"She's dead. That's bad; what's worse is she's got a piece of my shirt clutched firmly in one hand."

"Nice touch. How did it get there?"

"I don't know. I know it's mine because some goon took it off me about three hours before I found the body." He faced me, but his eyes were checking out the park and the street beyond. I waited for him to tell the story his way.

He shifted his attention back to me. "The blond—her name is, was Marilyn Wyte—called yesterday. She knew I was watching her, and she wanted to talk. She wouldn't say any more than that, just asked me to come to her apartment at two o'clock this afternoon."

"How did she know you were watching her?"

Peter shrugged, "I don't know. I must have been a bit less careful than I thought."

Peter was good at surveillance. Another professional might have spotted him, but it seemed highly unlikely that anyone else would have and even more unlikely that an ordinary honest-but-indiscreet secretary would have been able to find out his identity and how to contact him.

Peter continued. "The call was about ten-thirty. A little later, maybe around eleven, two thugs paid me a visit. They had guns, and they slapped me around a bit and warned me that I'd better mind my own business. They asked some questions that I didn't answer, but they weren't anxious enough for answers to work me over. Mostly, they just sat around looking menacing and killing time.

"Shortly before one o'clock they repeated their threats, tied me up and left. On the way out, one of them grabbed my shirt, a credit card, and some other clothes. You know where a piece of the shirt ended up; I'm guessing the rest of it is covered with bloodstains and stuffed someplace in the dead girl's apartment where even a cop couldn't miss it.

"I should have gotten suspicious when they did a second-rate job of tying me up. I was rushing so hard to get to the meeting, I didn't stop to wonder why it was so easy to get free."

"So you got there with just enough time to make your meeting and no alibi for the past two-and-a-half hours," I observed.

"Neat, huh?"

"Cause of death?" I asked.

"Her throat was slit, and from the look of her face, she'd taken quite a beating before. It wasn't a pleasant scene."

"I can see why you have no desire to see the police right now."

As if on cue, a police car cruised by on the other side of the park. Peter turned toward me. "Keep an eye on the black-and-white," he ordered. The car turned the corner and disappeared.

"Gone," I reported.

Peter shifted his attention back to the street. "Obviously I was set up. What I don't know is why or by whom."

"There's one obvious candidate," I pointed out. "Your client."

Peter shook his head. "She didn't care about the other woman; she's the one who wanted the divorce."

"Do you always believe what your clients tell you?" I asked a bit sarcastically.

Peter smiled ruefully. "You have to know her. She's just not the type."

"Come on, Peter, there is no type. How well do you know this woman?"

I knew the answer, or thought I did. I remembered Peter's telling me of meeting an old classmate from Stanford at a party during the summer. She was married, and her husband was wealthy. Peter had described her as wearing a diamond the size of a small boulder and enough other jewelry to make a Brinks guard nervous.

She'd been more than a little interested in the fact that he'd become a private investigator and was full of questions about his work. Lots of women suffer from romantic fantasies about private investigators, but she came on more like a client than a groupie.

She'd asked him to meet her for lunch the next day, he'd agreed, and they'd ended up at a little greasy spoon where she wouldn't meet anyone she knew. She wanted a divorce but was afraid her husband would take the kids if she went to court. She knew he was fooling around and wanted Peter prove it, to give her an edge in the custody fight.

Peter seemed to be considering the question of just how well he knew his client. "I haven't seen her for fifteen years, and people change, but not that much. It's not just what she was like then; it's what she's like now.

"She was tense and strung out when we met, and when I told her I don't do divorces, she went to pieces on me. In grad school, she was a together lady, bright, outgoing, self-assured without being stuck up. Today she looks like a classic battered wife—no self-confidence, full of fear, a lot of raw pain. She says he's never beaten her, but I wouldn't bet on it. Whatever he's done, it's had the same effect. I couldn't turn her down."

No, I thought, of course you couldn't.

Anyone who knew Peter would know he couldn't turn away from someone in pain, especially someone helpless. It was a part of him I loved, but it also made him vulnerable. I wondered if Peter's client was really as helpless as she'd appeared.

"Besides," Peter continued, "it wasn't Marilyn Wyte she asked me to watch. It was another woman. Susan— that's the client, Susan Clayton—gave me a phone number. It wasn't Marilyn Wyte's; it belonged to another woman, a good-looking brunette who's a secretary in the husband's computer company. She lived in one of those 'luxury' apartments that keep sprouting like toadstools along the freeway just south of Daly City.

"I watched her for a while; then I watched the husband. He's a real Don Juan. In the week I watched him, he visited five different girls—an impressive record for anyone over eighteen, especially when you figure that he's running a highly successful computer firm on the side. The dead girl in Palo Alto was obviously his favorite. I decided to concentrate on her. I had Eileen move in near her and try to strike up a relationship."

Eileen was Peter's enthusiastic but inexperienced assistant. I had a hunch she wouldn't enjoy divorce work any more than Peter did, but she'd be good at getting people to talk.

Peter's attention had shifted to the area around us. I understood now why he was so cautious. I knew what the criminal justice system would think of what he'd just told me—life without parole at best.

"How about the wife?" I asked. "Will she support your explanation of why you were interested in the girl?"

Peter grimaced. "I'm not counting on it. She was scared when I saw her, and she's going to be a whole lot more scared when she finds out her husband's mistress has been murdered. There's a good chance she'll clam up and pretend she never saw me."

I'd had the same thought. "Have you got any friends in the police on the Peninsula?"

"No one who'd stick his neck out for me. And I can't exactly ask the San Francisco cops for a reference."

I winced at the allusion to my ex-husband. "If you're referring to Dan, you needn't worry. He wouldn't let personal matters affect his job. Besides that was over and our divorce was almost final before I met you." I wondered for the thousandth time when the past finally stops being part of the present.

Peter was too involved in his own concerns to notice the irritation in my voice. "It may be over for you," he said, "but I'm not so sure about him. He and I never got along too well, even before you were in the picture. I don't think he'd lose any sleep over sending me to Quentin."

The gray clouds of fog had rolled in from the ocean, obscuring the late afternoon sun and chilling the air. I shivered, and Peter moved closer to put his arm around me.

"What are you planning to do now?" I asked.

"Well, I'm a bit limited by the fact that I'm starring on the evening news."

"What can I do?" The offer came automatically, before I could think about how much I did not want to become involved with people who killed other people.

"I could use your help on a couple of things," he said. "I don't think that either one is dangerous, but you can never be completely sure. I need a contact with the local cops to find out if they've come up with anything; and I need someone to go see Eileen.

"She's hiding at my cabin in Ben Lomand, and she says she knows something that might be useful. She's fairly new to this business, and she's probably scared to death. The best thing would probably be to put her on a plane and send her home to her parents."

"Her testimony is the only evidence you have that your interest in Marilyn Wyte was professional," I pointed out.

"By itself, her testimony won't do much for me. It'd just draw attention to her. She'll be safest back with her parents," he repeated.

"Macho man," I commented dryly.

"What?"

"You're playing macho man. You've already decided what's best for her without even consulting her. Have you considered it might be more devastating to run home than to stay here?"

Peter frowned and considered what I'd said. I had to give him credit for that; most men would have dismissed it outright.

"OK, it's not my place to send her home. Can you find someplace safe for her to stay if she doesn't want to go home?"

"I suppose so," I responded reluctantly. Great move, I thought, now I get to baby-sit Eileen. "Any idea what kind of information she has?"

Peter paused and his expression became positively grave. "I don't like getting you involved in this, and I don't want you to take on any more than seeing the cops and Eileen. This isn't your type of case. We're not dealing with nice polite corporate types. These guys are real thugs."

I swallowed my irritation at the last remark. I wasn't enthusiastic about getting involved with people who cut women's throats, but I resented Peter's suggestion that I couldn't handle the situation. "I'll be careful," I promised. "I just hope you will be, too. Now that you've been identified

as the prime suspect, the murderers might find it convenient
for you to disappear—permanently."

"Yeah, I've thought of that."

"Ben Lomand might not be a bad place for you to spend
time."

"While I wait for them to fit the noose? No thanks. I'm
planning on visiting some old friends who may be able to
give me a line on the jokers who grabbed me."

I didn't ask who the friends might be. Knowing Peter,
they could be anyone from former Weathermen to drug
dealers to Hell's Angels, or they could be college professors
or cops. In something over forty years he'd managed to
amass a strange assortment of friends, whose only common
characteristic was a respect and even a fondness for Peter.
He explained his unlikely set of friends with "I don't try to
change people, and I don't have to like everything about
them to appreciate the good parts."

My friends were considerably more conventional, but
though many wore uniforms, none worked on the Peninsula.
"I'll contact the Palo Alto police. I can't see them putting
out much effort to check on other suspects when they have
such an outstanding candidate, but I'll try to encourage them
in that direction."

I shivered again. In typical San Francisco manner, the
weather had moved from warm sun to bone-chilling fog.
"I'm freezing, Peter; let's go sit in my car."

My blue Volvo sedan was the only car left in the parking
lot. Peter patted it with mock affection. "Ah, the trusty blue
bus," he intoned.

"Don't knock my car." Peter had been teasing me for
months about buying a new car. It was reassuring to return

to the familiar repartee, a moment's respite from grim reality.

"I like my Volvo. I like the fact that no one notices it. I like the way it drives, and most of all I like the fact that it's the safest thing next to a Mack truck."

"It mystifies me that a woman who's practically obsessed with safety would go into detective work," Peter commented as he folded his six-foot frame into the car. "Doesn't it seem a bit inconsistent to you?"

"I am a woman of many contradictions."

"That's what I love about you."

"Keeps you on your toes."

"Yeah, but that's not my favorite position."

"Not much chance for that in jail. But back to business, Peter. If I'm going to talk to the police, I don't want to know where you're staying, but I will need to get in touch with you. Any suggestions?"

"Call LeRoy, he'll know where to get me."

LeRoy Hayes was one of Peter's friends from Haight-Ashbury days. Like Peter, he'd been a bit older and wiser than the flower children. And like Peter, he'd spent his time trying to translate their creed of peace and love into a viable new order. In the late sixties he'd cared for blissed-out hippies; in the 1980s he tended their younger brothers and sisters in a shelter for runaways. He retained his 1960s distrust of authority, and over the years he had developed a real talent for never knowing anything that might be remotely useful to the police.

"You realize he'll be one of the first people the police question."

"Yeah, but he doesn't mind lying," Peter grinned.

"True, and he does it so well."

"So do you, sweetheart, even if you don't like to admit it."

I smiled. "I make it a rule never to lie to my lover or the police."

"Puts me in great company, doesn't it?"

He leaned across the gearshift to kiss me. Peter's kisses were never short affairs; and they had a devastating effect on my ability to concentrate. As he slid his arm around me, I reluctantly pulled away. "Peter, this is one time I think we'd better put work before pleasure." I paused, trying to regain my train of thought. "If you'd like to make it a bit harder for people to recognize you, I have a friend who can help." I ran my fingers through his thick, wavy hair. "A permanent, maybe, a little make-up?" I tried not to chuckle at the thought.

Peter grimaced. "The cops aren't likely to recognize me unless they trip over me, and I want the people I'll be seeing to know who they're talking to."

"There are likely to be some other folks looking for you as well."

"So much the better. I want to make it real easy. The sooner I get a lead on them, the sooner things'll start to move. I'll call Eileen and tell her you'll be down tomorrow."

"Do you need me to get anything from your office? I mean, is there anything there that you wouldn't want the police to find?" I asked.

"I've already asked LeRoy to pick up the file with the information on the case. I want to keep Susan's name out of it if I can."

"How about your apartment?"

"Nothing there," he said, then frowning, "Oh, shit."

"What?" I asked.

"The SFPD will have to be involved in the search, and you know what that means."

I realized with chagrin exactly what it meant. Dan Walker would be searching Peter's apartment. I made a quick inventory of which of my things were there and felt a rush of schoolgirl embarrassment at having my ex-husband going through my lover's apartment. But that was the least of our problems. "When am I likely to hear from you tomorrow?" I asked.

"Probably in the evening. Just promise me that if Eileen does have a lead, you won't follow it up; that's my job."

"I promise," I said.

"God, I'd like to take you home tonight," he said in a tone that made it clear he couldn't. He leaned over, and gave me an uncharacteristically short and very gentle kiss. "Please be careful."

I returned the kiss. "I will if you will."

2

I was staring blankly into the refrigerator trying to figure out what sort of dinner might be assembled from the contents when the doorbell rang. The clock over the stove read 7:30—probably someone collecting money for another worthy cause.

I peered through the small window in the door. Instead of an idealistic college student armed with clipboard and pamphlets, I faced my ex-husband. He smiled, and waited for me to recover my composure.

I managed to smile back, open the door, and invite him in. Though I had seen Dan from time to time since our divorce, it was unsettling to confront him here, in what had been our home. I had the strange feeling that time had jumped backwards several years. He looked just like he had then—his dark hair still damp and curly from the shower he always took after working out, his clothes straight from

Brooks Brothers. The camel sports jacket was a new addition to his wardrobe, but he wore the same type of slacks and Oxford cloth shirt he'd favored when we were married. The shirt was open at the throat; his tie would be neatly folded in the right-hand pocket of his sports coat. He even smelled the same, the faint spicy fragrance of aftershave mingling with that of Irish Spring soap. It would be easier, I reflected, if he weren't still so damn attractive.

We sat down in the living room. He appeared comfortably at ease, but I'd known him long enough to catch the signs that told me otherwise.

"We had a call from the Palo Alto police this afternoon. It was about Peter Harman."

I nodded.

"I assume he's contacted you."

"Are you asking in an official capacity?" I asked.

He shook his head. "No, my interest is purely unofficial."

"I've spoken with him." I said.

Dan was annoyed by my silence. "Has he asked you for help?"

"He's asked me to check on some things."

The irritation was gone; Dan was absolutely cool and professional, a sure sign that things were serious. "How much do you know about the murder, Catherine?" he asked.

"I know Peter was framed." I told Dan about the thugs and the way the frame was set up.

Dan considered the information. Finally, he spoke: "I talked with one of the officers from Palo Alto about the case. It's a particularly nasty one, Catherine. The girl's throat was cut all right, but someone beat her up pretty badly before they killed her. The investigating officer says it's one of the worst cases he's seen."

He paused to let the last statement sink in.

"Peter said her face was bruised," I said at last.

"There was more . . ." He would have given me all the gruesome details, but I shook my head.

"I'll settle for the general picture, unless there's something that might be helpful in solving the case."

Dan made no effort to hide his annoyance. "I didn't come here to help you investigate this case, Catherine. I came to convince you to stay away from it. This is no corporate embezzlement scheme. The guy is a killer, and a sadistic one at that."

That was the second time today someone had suggested that this case was too tough for me to handle, and I was getting tired of it.

"Thank you for your concern, " I said icily.

"For God's sake, Catherine," Dan exploded. "Use a little common sense. Just for once—"

"Stop it, Dan," I interrupted. "Don't try to tell me how to live my life. I am not your wife anymore."

I was sorry as soon as I said it, and sorrier still when I saw the look of pain flicker across his face. No need to rerun the battle that had destroyed our relationship. We'd done that too many times.

The only way out had been divorce, and we'd done it quickly and cleanly, while we still cared for each other and before the ugliness of our battles destroyed what was good between us. The decision had saved us from the bitterness of a slowly withering marriage, but it had left us with an unresolved relationship—one in which attraction warred with the certain knowledge that we could never share a life together.

Dan was quick to regain control of himself. "You're right, of course; it's not my place to advise you."

Anger slipped into sadness and the sense of emotional exhaustion that our struggles always produced. "I appreciate your concern."

Dan smiled wanly.

"If it's any reassurance, Peter doesn't want me actively involved in the case either. I'm just getting some information for him."

I'd expected relief, but Dan looked uncomfortable again. He paused, then said, "Catherine, please try to understand what I'm about to say. Try to imagine that it's not me but someone else, someone not involved with us, who's asking the question." Another pause. "How well do you really know Peter Harman?"

I was stunned by the question, and by the unspoken suggestion that lay behind it. "Well enough to know he's not the killer," I replied.

Dan nodded. "I'm not saying he is. It's just that there's a lot of evidence pointing his way and only his word that he's innocent."

"Dan, you know Peter. Can you see him as someone who'd beat a woman and slit her throat?"

"I don't know him well enough to answer that."

"Well, I do," I said, "and I can tell you he couldn't do a thing like that. It's just not in his nature."

"I hope you're right. Just remember, when we pick up a guy like this, his neighbors can never believe he's a killer.

They'll tell you he was a regular guy—gentle, kind, a real prince. Often even the wife is fooled."

"Most neighbors and wives don't make their living assessing the criminal capacity of those around them," I pointed out. We were dangerously close to our old battleground. Time to change tactics. "Look at Peter's relationship with the street community," I argued. "He's been able to locate runaways that your men couldn't find. Those kids really trust him."

"I've considered that, Catherine, and I admire his work with those kids, but it's not going to help in a trial; in fact, it's apt to work against him. The prosecution will point out that runaways are ideal prey for a psychopath. They can disappear without anyone reporting it."

I was struck by the neat logic of his argument. No one really cared for street kids. To most adults, they were a bunch of misfits. The fact that Peter did care would be twisted to suggest a perverted motive.

"I know Peter didn't do it," I said, "just as I know you couldn't do something like that."

Dan nodded. "I'm sorry to have to suggest it," he said. "Someone killed that young woman in a particularly unpleasant manner. If it wasn't Harman, it was someone who knew a lot about him. Any way you look at it, your involvement in the case would put you in considerable danger."

I must not have looked sufficiently terrified. He let out a sigh of resignation. "Nothing I've said has had the least impact, has it? Damn, you're a stubborn woman." This time the irritation was softened by affection. "Well, since you're determined to be involved, I'll do whatever I can to help you."

"Thank you, Dan. That's very generous considering how you feel about Peter."

"I'm not doing it for him. I'm just trying to keep him from getting you hurt."

I attempted a wry smile. Same old Dan, always the protector. It's tough to be a knight in shining armor when the lady doesn't appreciate being rescued, I thought. Still, I wasn't above asking his help. "I could use some help with the Palo Alto police. Do you know anyone down there?" I asked.

"The man in charge of the investigation is Lou Martin. I talked to him a couple of hours ago."

"I could call him," I said, "but he'd pay more attention to you."

"I expect he'll tell you anything he'd tell me."

"Probably. But what I need right now is to make him aware that this thing's a frame-up. Otherwise, he won't follow up on evidence or leads that aren't connected to Peter."

Dan frowned. "It isn't going to be easy to get Martin to look for other suspects. Even if he believes you, and he probably won't, there's so much pointing to Harman that it'll be hard to break through automatic assumptions. They won't consciously disregard evidence, they just won't notice it."

"They'd be more apt to listen to you."

Dan looked pained. "You want me to call Martin and vouch for Peter Harman? I'm not even convinced he's innocent."

"Not vouch for him. Just let them know there's reason to consider a frame. Just get them to do their job."

"You realize I'd have to give them your name; they'd want to question you. The first question is going to be if you know where he's hiding."

"And I can honestly say that I don't."

"I figured that." He sighed and looked at his watch. "This is a big case. He may still be in his office." He walked into my study and sat down at the desk. He reached for the phone, called information and repeated a number then dialed it.

"Don't you ever write things down?" I asked, marveling at his memory.

"No." He hung up after a moment. "And I didn't forget it; I misdialed." He dialed again. "Lou Martin, please. Dan Walker, SFPD." A pause, then, "Hello, Lou. No, I don't have the report yet, but I'm calling about the case. I think I told you I know Harman somewhat, we have a mutual friend." He managed to keep the irony out of his voice when he said it.

"I've also worked with him a couple of times . . . No, I don't think he's the type. He's got a lot of bad points, but murder isn't one of them. Works a lot with runaways up here. The street people, especially the women, really trust him . . . Yeah, I know they're not the greatest references. But I'm not calling to serve as a character witness. I've got something for you. My friend who knows Harman has heard from him. He says that someone set him up."

There was a pause. Dan glanced up at me, but I couldn't read the look.

"Slow down, Lou. Her name is Catherine Sayler, and I've already gotten her to agree to come in tomorrow morning. Yeah, I asked if she knew anything about his where-abouts, and she doesn't."

Dan moved the receiver away from his ear a bit. The voice on the other end of the line did not sound pleased.

"She'll be in tomorrow, Lou. But in the meantime, I thought you should know that there's a chance it's a frame."

Dan frowned as he listened. "Yeah, it sounds pretty tight, and I know how it is when you're short-handed." The frown deepened. "Lou, I'm trying to warn you—I know Harman. He's worked for some big-name defense attorneys, and he'll be walking into that courtroom with one of the best. I'd hate to see a lot of good police work get thrown out because some smart-talking lawyer makes it look like you didn't handle the case properly. It's happened to us here enough times. I figured if I were in your place, I'd want to know if the jerk was going to claim a frame-up so I could prove we'd checked all the angles." The frown softened. "Yeah, sure. Glad to do it. I'll make sure my friend comes in. Good luck."

He was smiling as he hung up. In fact, he looked thoroughly pleased with himself. It was my turn to frown.

"I'm not sure whether to thank you or yell at you," I chided. "That sounded more like a hatchet job than anything else."

"You wanted them to check for leads, didn't you? That ought to get them to do it. Martin isn't the type of guy who responds well to suggestion. I figured he'd react much more positively to a fellow cop trying to help than to advice on how to conduct an investigation. Suburban cops can be very touchy about us big city types telling them what to do."

"You're right, as usual." I smiled. "Thanks, Dan, and I will go in tomorrow."

He rose and turned back toward the hall. "I don't suppose there's any way to talk you out of doing whatever you decide to do, but will you do me one favor, for old time's sake?"

For old time's sake was hardly a Dan Walker expression. How could I refuse? I nodded.

"Use me for back up. If things start to look tough or even potentially tough, give me a call."

"Hey, I don't plan to get close to anything tough, but if something goes bad, you'll hear from me."

"I learned a bit more. You want to know what they've got?"

"Of course."

What they had turned out to be about what Peter had guessed—a piece of paper with his phone number in the victim's handwriting found on her desk; his name, address and phone number in her address book; his shirt pocket in her hand, the rest of the shirt with bloodstains in the bathroom; and his pants with a credit card in her closet. It made a damn good case.

There was an awkward silence. Finally, I asked, "Would you like to stay for dinner?"

Dan smiled, but more from discomfort than from pleasure. "I think I'd best not."

I put my hand on his arm. "Dan, ex-lovers can still be friends."

"Yeah—" he smiled—"but that works best when you don't want to be more."

After Dan left, I ate a quickly-thrown-together meal and sat down with a cup of coffee, a pen, and a legal pad to consider the case. It was a ritual I'd repeated a hundred times, always in the evening. Dan had called it "mulling," and it was a process we'd enjoyed sharing during our relationship—sifting through the evidence, suggesting theories, testing hypotheses on each other. But it wasn't Dan I thought of tonight; it was the man who'd initiated me into the process and taught me the habits of thought that were second nature by now.

Keith Stone had been more than an employer and a mentor. He had been a second father. He was the best corporate security man in the business. He'd hired me as a favor to my dad, in a thinly disguised move to keep me from applying to the police academy, and he'd taught me a good deal more about investigative work than I'd have learned anywhere else.

In the beginning, I'd been little more than a secretary, but Keith had a quality rare in men of his generation—he took women seriously. As I established the fact that I was serious about my work he allowed me to become increasingly involved in his cases. His wife, Janet, had died three years before we met and his daughters both lived back East. I was new in San Francisco, with only a few casual friends. Work became my whole life for a while, and Keith became my family.

He'd trained me and allowed me to take increasing responsibility in the agency. He'd taught me about the corporate world—not just how it worked but how I had to work to be a part of it. I arrived in San Francisco looking like exactly what I was, the daughter of a policeman from

Denver, and after less than a year with Keith I could pass for a corporate vice president (though in those days the only women in executive suites carried steno pads).

Keith had given me something else. He had pointed out that a woman involved in criminal investigations should know something about self-defense. He'd suggested karate; I had chosen aikido, a gentler but no less deadly form of defense. What had begun as a physical discipline, a means to an end, had gradually become a way of life. It had offered me not only the skills to feel safe in a dangerous world but a view of life that was both practical and spiritual.

I forced my mind back to the case, and began by writing down everything I knew about it, which left far more questions than answers. The killing itself sounded like the work of a classic psychopath; but psychopaths don't go to the trouble of hiring people to frame someone else for the crime. The setup was too elaborate for either a crime of passion or insanity. The killing had to have been planned, probably well in advance. The thugs who held Peter were professionals; someone must have hired them.

Susan Clayton had the money to hire professional thugs. She'd claimed to need a private investigator to shadow her husband, but she could have been looking for a fall guy. I didn't buy Peter's unconditional endorsement of her veracity. One of the first things you learned in this business was a healthy skepticism for your clients' version of events. Peter knew that; it worried me that he could conveniently forget it.

Hugh Clayton also had the money to hire professional muscle, and if he knew that Peter was working for his wife, he had reason to arrange a frame-up. Motive was a problem. He didn't seem to have one.

Finally, it was always possible that the Clayton's were working together, their custody battle a clever fabrication to ensnare a target for the police. Too damn much was possible at this point. I reminded myself that Susan and Hugh Clayton made tempting suspects since we knew no one else connected with the girl. I didn't want to make the same mistake the police were making with Peter, deciding too quickly on a suspect and failing to investigate thoroughly for other possibilities.

I practiced a trick Keith had taught me and tried to look at the case from a different angle. I ran through the assumptions I had already made. I struck me that I'd assumed that the killer was after Marilyn Wyte and Peter had been a convenient scapegoat. But what if the killer was actually after Peter, and Marilyn Wyte was just a way to set him up? That would explain the care with which the frame was engineered. It might also explain the brutality.

I had avoided the details of what happened to Marilyn Wyte before she was killed, but Dan had made it clear that the crime had been particularly ugly. Murder was always awful, but a vicious, sadistic murder aroused particularly strong revulsion and antipathy toward the killer. When the details of this crime came out, the press, the public, and all but his closest friends would regard Peter as a monster.

But why Marilyn Wyte? If someone wanted to really hurt Peter, why go after a woman he didn't even know? Why not go after someone he cared for? Like me. The thought sent an uncomfortable feeling up my spine.

The pieces just didn't fit together. If Peter was the target, Marilyn wasn't the likely victim. And if Marilyn was the target, why had someone gone to so much trouble to frame Peter? Was one of them a random choice, or were they somehow linked in the killer's mind?

3

I walked out the door at 7:15 the next morning and discovered my nondescript blue Volvo decorated like a Muni bus. Some vandal had taken a can of spray paint to the hood and both sides. Scrawled across the driver's side was the message *Buy USA* while the passenger side was inscribed *Commie Sweeds*.

I noticed a piece of paper under the wiper and pulled it out. It was a Xeroxed attack on the traitors who throw American citizens out of work by buying foreign cars, and it was signed, *The Buy America Brigade*.

I wondered if my insurance covered acts of sabotage by patriotic lunatics; even if it did, I'd be out the deductible, which was probably about what a new paint job would cost. Worse yet, I would once again be at the mercy of my local Volvo dealer who worked with the speed of an antique restorer and charged similar prices.

The drive to Ben Lomand takes about an hour and a half. I had been looking forward to using the time to once again sift through what Peter and Dan had told me. Instead, I spent the first twenty minutes fuming about the Buy America Brigade. They couldn't possibly have chosen a worse time to strike. There was no way I could surrender my car to a garage right now, but I wasn't thrilled by the prospect of driving a car that only the blind could fail to notice.

I drove south on Highway 280, the freeway that cuts through the scenic foothills between the urban sprawl of the West Bay and the forested slopes of the Coast Range. I tried not to notice how many new look-alike boxy houses and tacky "luxury" apartment complexes had appeared since I first made this trip with Peter. Each time it took longer to get past the ugly suburban sprawl to the gold hills dotted with twisted black oaks.

I finally managed to focus my mind on the case and realized that my interest was not motivated solely by concern for Peter. Habit is a tricky thing and not easily overcome. He'd handed me a tantalizing puzzle, and I couldn't resist moving the pieces around to see how they fit together.

By the time I'd driven over the foothills and into the Santa Cruz mountains, I'd had plenty of time to go over the case. The only thing I knew was that I needed more information about a number of things. I'd known that the night before.

I took the Boulder Creek turnoff. The two-lane road lined with redwoods was my favorite part of the drive. It took forever to drive this stretch with Peter because he had a hundred favorite places to stop and was always finding new ones. He knew where every lane led, and the flowers that bloomed along each of them, which ones led to springs or streams, and which to stately groves of redwoods.

I turned up a dirt road, past several small cabins built in the 1940s and a larger, ranch-style house that would have been more at home in the suburbs of San Jose. At the end of the road, I turned left and parked beneath a row of redwoods that screened the small cabin just below them.

It looked as peaceful and quiet as usual. I didn't see Eileen's car, and my stomach knotted in warning. Peter or I would have parked away from the cabin, but I couldn't count on Eileen to have thought of that. The other explanation—that the killer knew she worked for Peter and had traced her to the cabin—was unlikely, but the possibility sent a rush of adrenaline through my system, straight to my stomach.

Ironically, I would have been in better control of myself if an attacker had stepped from behind a tree. I'd spent years in the dojo practicing calm in the face of attack. In a real attack, everything was suddenly very quiet inside, with no time for fear. Yet here in a situation that was probably quite safe, my heart was pounding.

I took several deep breaths to calm myself, and got out of the car. Irrational fear was no excuse for carelessness. I stayed behind the trees as I approached the cabin. I walked to where I could be seen from the door yet could easily duck behind the trees if necessary and called out, "Eileen, it's me, Catherine."

The door opened slowly and she peered out. I'd only met her once before, but I was struck by the alteration in her appearance. Eileen's hair was dark, almost black, but she had the fair skin of a blond. It was a striking combination, and I'd been impressed by her beauty. I remembered giving

Peter a bad time about hiring such an attractive assistant. The stress of the past twenty-four hours had drained the color from Eileen's face, transforming her natural fairness to pallor. Her unnaturally white skin, outlined by short dark hair, gave her an almost ghostly appearance.

"Catherine," she called, her voice betraying her relief. She stepped out to meet me.

I put my arm around her and gave her a hug, then led her into the cabin, and shut the door. She was frightened, all right; Peter'd been right about that. "Let me get you something to drink," I suggested. "I think there's brandy, probably tea and coffee, as well."

"I'd like some tea, please, herbal if you have it," she replied.

Herbal tea seemed a weak comfort; I'd have gone for the brandy in her place, but Eileen was definitely the herbal-tea type. I scrounged around and found a plastic bag marked peppermint; it smelled like peppermint and it looked like tea, so I tossed some in the tea strainer and put on the kettle.

A quick look in the refrigerator revealed that Eileen hadn't stopped to buy food. The remains of a Kentucky Fried Chicken dinner sat forlornly on the counter. There wasn't much in the cupboard, but I did manage to find an unopened box of Triscuits. The coffee tin had a bit of ground French roast left, (probably stale but still better than instant), so I was able to make myself a decent cup of coffee while Eileen's tea steeped.

I set the tea and Triscuits in front of Eileen. "How are you doing?" I asked.

She had been nervously picking at her fingernails, but stopped at the sound of my voice. "I'm okay." Her appearance contradicted her words.

"I think I might be rather shaken up if I were in your position," I prompted.

"Yes, well, I guess I'm pretty scared, really. I mean, I know I shouldn't be, but I'm . . . scared. I keep hearing things and thinking there's someone outside."

I nodded and realized there really wasn't much I could say. "Do you feel up to talking about Marilyn Wyte?" I asked.

Eileen seemed relieved. "Oh, yes," she said. She took a breath and began. "I've got something for you, but I don't know what it means. Tuesday night, two nights before she was killed, I got Marilyn to go drinking with me. She'd been real distant, but I guess I caught her at the right moment because she agreed to go out for a drink.

"Anyway, I steered the conversation to dating and how I only met married men. She made some disparaging remarks about men in general and went on about how the deck's stacked against women. It wasn't like a feminist thing, you know; it was more personal. Like she was pissed off about something. She is, was, a fairly heavy drinker, and she didn't hold it very well. By the third martini, she started in on how dumb men were and how women are smarter than their bosses but it doesn't matter because nobody cares how smart you are just how much money you have."

Eileen paused for breath and to see if I was following what she was saying. I nodded, and she continued. "Then, she leaned across the table and said something about how she wasn't going to spend her life as some man's secretary or even his wife. She said—and these are just about her exact words—'I'm getting out, and I'm going first class. I'm going to Mexico or Spain and buy a big house and live the good life.'

"I pretended I didn't believe her, like she was joking. I went, 'It's going to take a long time to save that kind of money.' And then she said, 'Not for me. I'm leaving next—' At that point she caught herself and laughed, acted like she was just kidding. She avoided me the next day, so that was our last conversation. I had a clear sense that she was planning on leaving soon—a week, maybe a month, no longer."

"Any clues about where the money was coming from?" I asked.

Eileen shook her head. "No, but I'd bet it was coming from one of the men who visited her. Clayton wasn't her only man, you know. In the weeks I lived there, she had a real active social life."

Things were getting interesting. "How many different men?" I asked.

"Four, besides Clayton, maybe more."

"Did they take her out?"

"Sometimes, but often they stayed home. Only one ever stayed the night. Sometimes she came home in the afternoon with one man and went out that night with another."

"Did you manage to get any names?"

"No, but I did get the license numbers of all four cars."

Peter had been right about Eileen. She did have promise as an investigator. She'd known enough to pay attention to details even when they weren't clearly related to the case she was working on. "Nice work, Eileen," I said. "That gives us a good place to start."

"What do you make of what she told me?" Eileen asked.

I wasn't sure. With five men, sometimes two a day, prostitution was a possibility, but not a likely one. Hooking's a business where profit depends on volume. Successful call girls don't waste valuable time working as secretaries.

Clayton was wealthy enough to support a mistress. If the other four were also rich, Marilyn could have been making her money that way. On the other hand, a man supporting a mistress would expect to spend longer with her than a couple of hours once or twice a week. And he wouldn't want to share her with a bunch of other men.

That could be the motive, of course—jealousy. One found out about the others and killed her for her infidelity. But the murder had been planned too carefully for a crime of passion.

Blackmail was another good possibility, but it seemed strange that she was seeing so many men. A blackmailer doesn't usually take on that many at once. Still, blackmail was a better motive for murder than the need to get rid of a mistress; and if the stakes were high enough, it'd provide a reason for framing Peter. The frame would be a good way of diverting attention so the police wouldn't look too deeply into the victim's social life.

I ran through the various scenarios for Eileen, developing my thoughts as I did so. None of them really satisfied me, but blackmail came closest to fitting the facts.

I'd forgotten that Eileen didn't know the details of Marilyn's death, and cursed myself for not being more sensitive when I saw her reaction to them. She might have the instincts for this kind of work, but she was a long way from emotionally ready to deal with the realities. She shivered and her pale face seemed even whiter than before. Hesitantly, she asked, "Catherine, do you ever get scared?"

We were back to that subject again. I should have known I couldn't ignore it. "Of course," I answered truthfully, "I'd be a fool not to in this business."

"How do you handle it? I've never felt like this. Every sound makes me jump. My stomach's so knotted up that I don't think I could eat."

She wanted a few reassuring words, I suppose. But words don't change the way you feel inside. That only changes when you learn to control the fear. Aikido had done that for me. But those skills took months to start and years to perfect, and Eileen wanted an answer now.

"One way to handle the fear would be to get you away from here, to someplace you'd feel safe," I suggested. "Peter said you have family in the Midwest."

I'd expected relief; instead, I saw dismay. "I don't want to go home." Eileen said vehemently. "I hate feeling scared, but I don't want to go home."

She had me there. In her anguished cry, I heard my own voice, years earlier, my own conflict between the desire to be independent and the urge to have someone else care for and protect me. "I think I understand," I said.

She looked at me timidly. I could feel something coming. "Do you think—that is, is there any way I might be able to work with you?"

That caught me by surprise. I'd jumped on Peter for automatically wanting to send her home, but I certainly wasn't prepared to take on an inexperienced assistant.

Eileen was watching me closely, and she was astute enough to read my expression. "I don't mean in the field. I know I'm not up to that. But maybe in the office. Maybe I could help check on the men who visited Marilyn."

I was becoming more impressed with Eileen by the moment. With both my assistants, Chris and Jesse, working on other cases, I could use some help. Still, I wasn't anxious to do any hand-holding; and Eileen could easily be more of a burden than a help.

"You'd be safest here." I pointed out.

"I'd be safest in Ohio with my mother, but I don't want to be safe that way. I want to be a detective—at least I want to try to be one. I want to find out if I can do it."

"And if you can't?"

"I guess I'll go back to Ohio."

She said the last with a little smile that suggested she was not quite serious.

I laughed. "No need for such drastic action yet," I assured her. "I'll have space for you in my office for a couple of weeks. One of my assistants is in Seattle on another case, and I don't expect her back for a while. Where do you live?"

"Berkeley."

"You should be all right there. But I'll put you up in my apartment until we're sure yours is safe. I don't want you down on the Peninsula until the killers are in custody."

Eileen's look of relief made it clear that she had no desire to return to the Peninsula. "Oh, thank you, Catherine," she exclaimed. "Shall I get my things?"

I nodded. Eileen disappeared into the bedroom and re-emerged after a moment with a parka and a rather battered leather purse.

"I didn't see a car. Do you have one?" I asked.

Eileen nodded. "I parked it on the next road in case the murderer knew what it looked like."

"Good thinking." I liked Eileen. I'd always regarded prudence as a virtue. It was a good quality in a colleague, especially in this line of work. "Do you know your way around San Francisco?" I asked.

"Pretty well."

I pulled out a business card. "Can you find this place?" I asked, pointing to the Divisidero Street address. "It's several blocks north of Geary. My apartment is only a few blocks away on Clay." I wrote the address on the back of the card.

"Don't go back to the Palo Alto apartment or your own. Go to my office. My secretary's name is Amy Montgomery. I'll call ahead so she'll be expecting you. You'll need some clothes; she'll take you shopping. My clients are generally large corporations, so around the office, we're a pretty straight-looking bunch. I'd like you to get yourself a good suit and several blouses. Amy'll take care of paying for things with the company card." I reached in my purse and pulled out the envelope I'd planned to give Eileen to get her back to Ohio. "There's two hundred dollars in the envelope; it should take care of gas and other incidentals."

Eileen looked a bit dazed. I realized I might be moving a bit fast for her. But she'd have to be able to keep up if she was going to work on the case. "Have you ever used a computer?" I asked.

Eileen recovered her composure. "Sure."

"Have you done background searches for Peter?"

"He's shown me how, but I've never done one on my own. I've always worked under his supervision."

"That's fine. I sometimes pay another agency to do background checks, but this time we'll do most of the work ourselves. My assistant, Jesse, can tell you what to do and how to do it. I'll call him when we leave here and get him started checking out the car license numbers. We'll run them through SCI—that's an information broker. It usually takes twelve to twenty-four hours to get the information, so there won't be much on that today, but you two can start checking on Marilyn Wyte. I'll meet you back at my apartment around six-thirty."

Eileen nodded. "Where are you going now?"

I told her that after I called Jesse, I had to stop by the Palo Alto Police Department to see Lou Martin.

"Are you going to tell them about the four men?" she asked.

I shook my head. "Not yet. It's possible that they'd dig up something useful, but it's more likely they'd just do perfunctory interviews and put everyone on their guard. Besides, it'd be impossible to keep you out of it if I told them."

"What *are* you going to tell them?" she asked.

"Just what Peter told me. That doesn't require any lies or bending of the truth. If I tried to tell part of your story, they'd sense I was holding out. I want as friendly a relationship as possible with Lou Martin.

"I'm not sure where I'll be after that, but if you need me before six-thirty, leave a message at the San Francisco Aikido Dojo. I teach a class there at five o'clock."

"Aikido?" Eileen asked.

"It's a martial art, a bit like judo. I started studying it for self-defense, but it's a lot more than that to me now. They'll take a message and see that I get it at the dojo. Are you ready to go?"

Eileen nodded and headed for the door. I caught her arm as she reached for the doorknob. "Don't," I said. "You're feeling safer now. Don't confuse that with *being* safer. You had reason to be afraid an hour ago; you still do."

Eileen stopped, looking confused and alarmed.

I didn't think there was anyone out there, but I didn't want Eileen developing a false sense of security that would make her careless. Trouble happens when you least expect it, and as long as Eileen was involved in investigative work, she'd better learn that.

One of the fringe benefits of my job was the effect it had had on my awareness. When I started, I'd walked through life in a half-awake state, daydreaming as I walked down the street, always thinking about something other than what was happening around me. Keith Stone and my instructors at the dojo had broken me of that habit. Both constantly reminded me to pay attention to everything around me and to keep my mind focused on present experience.

Peter was also a real "stay in the moment" person, and I had the feeling he'd always been that way. With Keith, intense awareness seemed a long-established habit of mind. Picked up on the job, it had become so much a part of him that he couldn't lay it aside.

But Peter was different. He studied the first crocus or the fog flowing in through the Golden Gate with the same intensity he applied to his work. Walking down the street with him was an adventure, full of serendipitous discoveries.

I was suddenly aware of how much a part of my life he had become and had to push aside a muddle of disturbing emotions. I was definitely not staying in the moment.

I locked the door from the inside and led Eileen to the back door. "This one is safer," I explained. "The trees are close to the house so there's cover if you need it. I don't expect there's anyone out there, but there's no point in taking unnecessary chances."

I slid the door open slightly and listened. Then I told her to go to my car. "If anything happens, fall to the ground."

She nodded. Her face was like a mask, and I felt a pang of guilt for scaring her. Keith had done that to me often enough, pointing out careless acts that could have had dire consequences. Something in her face reminded me of the vulnerability I'd felt then. Youth wasn't nearly so wonderful as the commercials made it out to be.

Eileen forced herself to walk out the door and up to my car. I locked the door and followed.

"I'll take you to your car, then make my good-citizen visit to the Palo Alto police." She didn't smile, but then, she didn't have much reason to.

4

The Palo Alto City Hall is a high-rise by Peninsula standards, which means that it's about eight stories instead of forty. The Police Department is discreetly hidden behind it in a one-story building screened by street trees. The good citizens of Palo Alto like their protectors to keep a low profile.

I introduced myself to the desk sergeant, a thin young man with a bored expression and a sadly wispy mustache. I asked for Lou Martin. When I added that my visit was related to the Marilyn Wyte case, he became considerably less bored and somewhat more efficient.

Martin was a middle-aged man, solidly built, slightly rumpled—the kind of man who only wears a coat to and from the office. Two things about him stood out—his eyes and his voice. The eyes were a pale blue but very intense, with a kind of unsmiling watchfulness, and the voice was unusually soft. There was nothing soft in his manner though, and I found my new role of "friend of the felon" far from pleasant.

Our meeting went pretty much as I'd expected it to. Martin asked a lot of questions, most of which I couldn't answer. I asked some questions, most of which he didn't answer. He wasn't openly hostile, but I had the distinct feeling that he'd have happily offered me a few days in a cell to improve my character.

It was an uncomfortable position to be in, especially since I'd always worked closely with the police. I felt awkward and got through the interview as quickly as possible.

I was anxious to have Jesse get started on tracing the license numbers, but he'd been out when I called from Ben Lomand. I found a phone booth at a service station and called again. This time he was in.

Jesse Price had been with the agency for two years. He'd walked into the office one day and announced that he wanted to work for me. He didn't look like much, a skinny black kid in a brand-new suit, but he'd been sent to me by a lawyer I respected and to whom I owed a favor. The lawyer discovered Jesse at Golden Gate University, a night school where with some brains, considerable amounts of endurance and lots of Nodoze, secretaries and mail clerks could transform themselves into lawyers and junior executives. Jesse was working on a law degree, but that was only a small part of his plans.

Jesse came to me knowing exactly what he wanted. He told me right off that he wanted to work for me for five years, at the end of which time he intended to move on to take over as Chief of Corporate Security for a Fortune 500 company. It took only a short time for me to discover that he had the brains to match his ambition.

He learned quickly, and as soon as he mastered one subject, he was on to the next. His current passion was computers, and he was already the expert in our office on the subject. I was grateful to have someone to hold my hand and teach me the ins and outs of WordStar and Lotus 1-2-3, but Jesse's real interests ran to the less legally sanctioned uses of computers.

He wasn't a hacker; but he had managed to gain the acceptance of a bunch of hackers on the Peninsula. He spent weekends with them and on Monday mornings was full of stories of their latest escapades. I alternated between being appalled by their exploits and fascinated by the possible applications of their discoveries.

Jesse's voice came on the line. "Hi, boss lady. What can I do you for?"

I gave him the license numbers and explained what I wanted.

"Bad news," he said. "I just called SCI on something else. Their computer's down, and they already have a forty-eight-hour backup."

"Damn. We need those names as soon as possible."

"You could get a cop to run them for you," Jesse suggested.

"I was hoping to avoid that. Those numbers are evidence in a criminal case, and I wouldn't want them passed on to the Palo Alto Police."

"Well, there *is* another way," Jesse hinted. The tone of voice told me it was probably illegal. "I have friends on the Peninsula who know the password that a certain police department uses to tap into the DMV computer. One dude ran his ex-wife's license number; it works."

I restrained myself from lecturing Jesse on appropriate procedures or the high price of illegal activity. After all, it was Peter's life we were dealing with. "You're sure it works? If we got caught, we'd lose our license, maybe even end up doing some time at the state's expense," I pointed out grimly.

"It works," Jesse assured me.

"How's your schedule? Can you take time to get the password today?"

Jesse considered for a moment. "I have to drive to San Jose to interview the accountant in the Eisley case, and I have a meeting at four in Daly City, but I could probably fit it in."

"Skip the accountant if necessary. The password's more important," I said. "Are you free this evening?"

"For you, always."

"I'll call you after dinner, and you can introduce me to the marvels of the computer age."

"My pleasure. Claire'd probably appreciate it if we could meet after eight o'clock. Is that possible?"

"How about nine?"

"You're on."

I still had several hours before my class at the dojo, and it seemed a shame to waste them. I decided to pay a visit to an old friend at Stanford. Dr. Leo Goldberg was in the Electrical Engineering Department, but while he dwelt in the ivory tower, he always had an ear to the ground. He had been a roommate of Keith's in college and considered himself something of an amateur sleuth. He devoured mystery books, and his first question was always, "Working on an interesting case?" Keith never discussed cases with outsiders, except for Leo.

I'd seen Leo a number of times since Keith's death. In addition to being a good friend, he was an excellent source of information about what was happening on the Peninsula. He consulted for a number of high-tech firms, and his natural curiosity and outgoing manner made him a man who asked lots of questions and got lots of answers. If he'd been a woman, he would probably have been considered a gossip. As it was, he was regarded as something of an expert on the state of the computer industry.

A long palm-lined drive led from the town of Palo Alto to the buff sandstone buildings of the main quadrangle of Stanford University. Set at the end of the drive, the Spanish style buildings with their red tiled roofs had a jewel-like quality. They called it "the Farm," but it had more the feeling of a very expensive private club. It always seemed a bit incongruous that Peter with his aggressively egalitarian views had actually been a graduate student at Stanford.

He explained it as primarily a means of avoiding the draft, but if that had been his entire motive, he could have stayed in Berkeley at the University of California. Instead, he'd enrolled in the English Department at Stanford.

As far as I could tell, he hadn't spent an inordinate amount of time studying. It was the late sixties and there were too many exciting things happening outside the classroom. But when he wasn't being cynical or hip, Peter spoke of both Stanford and his studies with a definite fondness. A part of him would have loved to be an English professor, but that part had long ago been beaten out by the social activist. I had to admit I was glad; the English professor might not have been nearly as much fun.

I drove around to the north side of campus to the Electrical Engineering Department. The nearest visitors' parking lot was only a few miles away. I parked amid the Porsches and BMWs and hiked to Leo's office. The door was open, and I peered into the room. In the midst of books and piles of papers sat Leo. He was talking on the phone, but he motioned for me to come in.

I scooped a pile of books off a chair and sat down. Leo hadn't changed much since I'd last seen him a few months ago. In fact, Leo hadn't changed much in the years that I'd known him. He'd always been a smallish older man with a glorious head of white hair and a slightly impish expression. If the roadmap of wrinkles on his face had deepened or expanded, I was never aware of it.

Leo ended his conversation and turned to me. "So, Catherine," he said, "more beautiful than ever. What're you working on?"

"What makes you think I'm working on something? Maybe I just stopped by for the pleasure of your company and to inquire after your lovely wife and daughters."

Leo smiled knowingly. "My lovely wife and daughters are fine. Rebecca has decided to specialize in pediatrics and Sarah is about to make me a grandfather for the second time. What more could a man ask for? Now you have the family news; you tell me what's happening in your life, then we can get down to why you're here, which I hope has to do with a case."

The main thing that had been happening in my life was Peter, and any other time I would have enjoyed telling Leo about him. But today I passed over my personal life and responded, "Everything is fine with me; the agency is flourishing. I may even have to hire another assistant."

"Keith would be proud of you," he said. He was astute enough to notice that I had skipped over my personal life but polite enough not to ask why. "You are here on a case?" he asked pointedly.

"I am," I admitted. "I need some background information on some people in the industry, and I thought you might be able to help. Do you know a Hugh Clayton?"

"Hugh Clayton? Sure, he's a pretty big man down here."

"How well do you know him?" I asked.

"I've met him a number of times, been on a panel with him once, but he's not a personal friend if that's what you mean."

Leo made little effort to hide his curiosity. I was going to have to give him a reason for my questions. I didn't want to lie, and I couldn't tell him the truth, which left me in an awkward position. Finally I said, "I need some background information about him because his name's come up in a case. I can't tell you more without breaching client confidentiality."

It wasn't much of an answer to Leo's unspoken questions, but he knew it was all he was going to get. "Will you tell me what you know about him?" I asked.

Leo looked disappointed, but he nodded. "He's president of Clayton Electronics, a middle-sized firm that supplies a variety of electronic goodies to the computer industry. He's something of a phenomenon around here. He knows ten times what I do, and he has this extraordinary ability to put it all together and make projections about what's going to happen. He'll wink and tell you to watch for a new product announcement from so-and-so; and by golly, a couple of days later, there it is. I sure wish I had his crystal ball."

"I understand he's quite wealthy," I said.

"I expect so," Leo replied. "I don't really know anything about his financial situation, but on top of owning a successful business, I'd guess he's made a fortune in investments. That ability to see trends and anticipate what's coming up is a great asset if you have a bit of venture capital lying around."

"What can you tell me about his company?"

"Ah, now there's a story that'd intrigue you. Do you know what I mean by the 'gray market'?"

I shook my head.

"Well, it's a Silicon Valley invention. It's called the gray market because it's not quite as dirty as the black market but not totally clean either."

Leo, always the consummate storyteller, paused for effect, then went on. "You see, the high-tech companies depend on a number of other companies to supply them with the parts that go into their products, and often there are a number of companies buying the same part. If Xerox and Apple both need the same chip at the same time, someone can end up short, and ending up short can cost millions of dollars.

"It's not that uncommon for a company to discover that a million-dollar deal is about to fall apart because they can't get one part that they need. That's where the gray market suppliers come in. They can sometimes get what you need, for a price. Now if you need a chip real bad, you don't ask questions about where it came from. And the parts supplier probably doesn't ask whoever supplies him too many questions, either."

A young man who looked about twelve poked his head in the door at that point and asked a question. He wanted to discuss his grade in the graduate seminar. It made me feel very old. Leo told the child-wonder to come back later and continued with his lecture.

"Where was I?" he asked, not really expecting an answer. "Ah yes, the gray market. Well, often the source of the parts is perfectly legitimate—maybe somebody bought a batch of parts and has extras and sells them off, or maybe the supplier picked up a batch of chips when they were plentiful and cheap because he figured someday they'd be scarce and valuable. But sometimes, and my guess is it's not so unusual, the items are hot, as you say in the trade. They were stolen, and the parts supplier becomes the fence."

He could see he had my interest. Larceny is always a hot topic.

"You have to remember," he went on, "that the most valuable parts in the computer business are often the smallest. The central processing unit of a computer is a microchip that's not much bigger than my thumbnail. A guy can pick up a handful of the right chips and walk out the door with several thousand dollars in his pocket. And the place he walks to is the supplier."

"You make it sound incredibly easy," I protested. "Surely someone's watching those handfuls of chips, and I would expect the police would be monitoring the suppliers."

"This is a young industry, founded largely by men who were never comfortable with the Big Brother attitudes of big business. There's a feeling that if you crack down on employees too hard you'll alienate them and lose the kind of creative flow that's been so beneficial to the industry. Besides, in the beginning there was so much money that no one cared too much if guys were helping themselves to a little extra, as long as they didn't get too greedy. That's changing as companies get more established and as profit margins fall, but corporate security is still fairly new in a lot of these companies.

"As for pressure on the suppliers, there's a lot of ambivalence about that. After all, the same company that curses over the theft of its materials goes out and buys chips or parts that were probably stolen from someone else's warehouse. Time is money in this business, and it's worth a lot to people not to have to wait till the legitimate supply lines can kick up the part they need. The gray market provides a kind of grease that keeps the industry moving. No one's too anxious to monkey with that."

"And Hugh Clayton's involved in the gray market," I prompted.

"He was once. I don't know how much of his business is that now. I think his company produces much of the stuff it sells. I doubt that he ever knowingly handled stolen goods. I think Hugh's success came from the quality I described before, that ability to predict what's coming. You see, if you have a good idea of what people are working on, you have a clue as to what they might need. A man like Hugh knows what parts are likely to be in demand later on."

"Would he do something dishonest?"

Leo considered. "No, I really don't think so. I'm sure he's a tough businessman. When we have a conversation, I always have the vague feeling that I've told him more than he's told me, but I don't think he'd knowingly break the law."

"Do you know anything about Clayton's wife Susan?" I asked.

"Susan Clayton. Don't think I've ever met her."

"Would Miri know her?"

"I doubt that they've met."

"Miri knows lots of people," I prompted. "Would you mind calling and asking if she knows anything about Susan Clayton?"

Leo's eyes twinkled, "Are you suggesting," he asked, "that the girl that I married, the light of my life, is a gossip?"

"Never. I'm merely pointing out that she shares your formidable curiosity and interest in the affairs of the human race."

Leo was already punching the numbers into his phone. It was typical of him that he had scored a touch-tone phone while everyone else in the department remained in the Dark Ages of the rotary dial.

"Miri, hi, guess who's in my office? Catherine. No, not Bernie's Catherine, Keith's Catherine, the lady detective. Right. Listen, sweetheart, here's your big chance. Catherine needs some information for a case. Dig into your database and see if you know anything about Susan Clayton; she's Hugh Clayton's wife."

Miriam must have known something because Leo listened intently, nodding and grunting occasionally. Suddenly, his expression became very grave. He looked positively distressed.

He hung up and turned to me with the same worried expression. "You didn't tell me your friend Peter was in trouble," he said.

I was taken aback. "I didn't know you knew Peter," I answered.

"Miri and I met him last year at the open house you had at the agency. We spent the entire evening talking with him. An extraordinary young man! We discussed existentialism and Eastern mysticism. Best conversation I've had in ages. Miri says he's wanted for a murder in Palo Alto."

I hadn't expected Leo to know Peter or to be aware of the murder. He eschewed television and radio news and refused to read any paper except the *New York Times* and the *Wall Street Journal*. His acquaintance with Peter presented me with a dilemma. I'd already asked about Susan and Hugh Clayton, and Leo was sharp enough to suspect that they might somehow be connected with Peter's case. I didn't want that information to get out.

I began by explaining what I knew about the murder and the way Peter had been framed, carefully leaving out two facts: that Susan Clayton had hired Peter and that her husband had been seeing the dead girl. When I finished, Leo asked, "And Hugh or Susan Clayton is somehow involved in this?"

"Possibly," I answered truthfully. "I really can't tell you more than that, and it's extremely important that no one know I was even asking about them."

"Understood," Leo nodded thoughtfully. He was uncharacteristically subdued. Finally, he said, "I always thought it would be great fun to be involved in a case, but knowing people who are is actually very troubling. I don't know Peter well, but I liked him very much. Tell him I'll help if there's any way I can."

"I will," I promised.

"I have to tell you I can't imagine Hugh Clayton involved in a violent crime," he offered.

"Most likely he's not," I said. "Did Miri have anything to say about Susan Clayton?"

"Oh, yes. I was so upset by hearing about Peter, I completely forgot. She says Susan is a very nice, very bright lady but she has 'problems.' She's had a couple of breakdowns. Miri doesn't know her well; but they're both on a fund-raising committee for the Stanford Children's Hospital, and Susan's been away for extended periods a couple of times.

"It happens down here, you know, especially to women about her age. They're really too bright and ambitious to be housewives, but they grew up and got married before women's lib. Once the kids are in school, there's too much time and too little worthwhile to do. That's Miri's analysis anyway. Makes sense to me. I'd go crazy sitting around a house all day."

It made sense to me, too; but I needed to know more about the breakdowns. If they were really breakdowns, they could involve paranoia, which would cast considerable doubt on Susan's story to Peter. Mental illness was as good an explanation for her shattered appearance as either physical or mental abuse. On the other hand, "breakdowns" could be a convenient explanation for periodic disappearances to recover from physical abuse. It wouldn't do for the wife of a well-to-do businessman to show up with bruises or a black eye.

Either way, Miri's information about Susan Clayton fit better with Peter's maiden-in-distress story than with my Brigid O'Shaughnessy scenario. Leo had given me a lot to think about, and I needed time to mull it over. I told him that, and left without the usual small talk that marks the ending of a conversation. I was thankful that he understood and would not regard my abrupt departure as a lapse of good manners or, worse yet, a personal slight.

5

I arrived at the dojo at 4:30. As I slipped out of my shoes and bowed, it was as if I moved into a different world. The large white room was flooded with late afternoon sunlight that poured in through the tall windows and shimmered on the white, mat-covered floor. At the far end sat the room's only ornamentation, a black-and-white photograph of a distinguished elderly Japanese man with a small vase of bright orange nasturtiums in front of it. I bowed to the tiny shrine, a gesture of respect to Morihei Uyeshiba, the founder of aikido.

Somehow this room always felt peaceful, even when it was filled with people who appeared to be locked in mortal combat. At the moment there were six pairs of students on the mat. All wore loose-fitting white pants and jackets tied with either brown or black belts; several also wore the black *hakama*, a long skirt-like garment reserved for women and for those who had attained the black belt. This was the advanced class, and I'd missed it again.

I watched the pairs work together. To an inexperienced observer, it would have seemed a brutal battle. In reality the practice was closer to a carefully choreographed dance. One partner attacked, the other practiced a defense. Where the partners were roughly equal in ability, it was a contest, but where one was more experienced, the attack was moderated to be just difficult enough to challenge without overwhelming the less proficient partner.

I looked over the group, wondering which of them might be willing to wait around until after my class for a practice session. On the far side of the mat I noticed a small woman with an Ace bandage on her ankle. It was Janet Halliday, a student from the first class I'd taught at the dojo. I knew she'd injured her ankle slightly last week. The fact that she was on the mat before it was completely healed was as much a badge of her growth as the brown belt she wore around her waist.

Janet had first come to the dojo to learn aikido so that she would feel safer on the street, but she was terribly afraid of being injured during practice. During one session she was paired with a particularly inept partner who accidentally hit her in the face. She fled from the mat, and sat out the rest of the session. I was afraid she'd give up aikido on the spot, but when I spoke with her afterwards, she was remarkably calm. She told me, "I've spent my life being scared of having somebody hit me in the face; it wasn't nearly as awful as I'd built it up to be."

Now she was a brown belt, and an injury was just part of life. Watching Janet reminded me that there was a reason I'd chosen to teach the beginning classes.

There was a loud clap, and the partners froze in their positions, then bowed to each other and knelt on the mat. They lined up in front of Frank Bowden, the head teacher or *sensei*; he knelt facing them, and they bowed to each other, then to the shrine, and practice was over.

As the class left the mat, I hurried over to see if I could talk a couple of people into sticking around till my class was over. I was in luck; Alex Ichazio and two of his friends were planning to stay to practice for Alex's black belt exam and would be willing to work out with me when I finished teaching. If I couldn't work with the advanced class, working with Alex and his friends was the next best thing.

For some reason the five o'clock class always seemed to attract a disproportionate number of Bruce Lee fans. Some days I felt like I spent most of the hour trying to keep them from injuring themselves. Today we were working on shoulder strikes, and there were at least three young men who went into the strike like kamikaze pilots and dissolved into Jell-o as soon as their opponent tried to throw them. I clapped, and they knelt where they were.

"Remember as you practice, the role of *uke*, the attacker, is as important as the role of defender. When you're uke, you have to fall; what becomes important is how you do it. Never let yourself be thrown. Be in control of your movement at all times. When you go down, throw yourself. Direct your own energy." I looked around at their faces, trying to see if I was getting through at all.

"We talk about aikido as a way of living. How you deal with the role of uke here in the dojo is how you deal with difficult situations in life. You can't choose not to be fired or laid off or not to have someone you care about leave you, but you can control your reaction. You can guide the fall so that you come up ready to deal with whatever comes next."

One of the kamikazes was looking at me intently; maybe there was hope after all. I went on. "Some of you are working much too hard on the throws. We're working with energy and balance, not muscle here. If you have to rely on muscle, you're not doing the throw correctly." I called to Alex, who was working on the next mat, "Will you help me demonstrate, please?"

Alex was a good choice for my purposes. He outweighed me by close to a hundred pounds. We bowed to each other. "Attack when you're ready," I instructed.

He stood still for a moment, then sprang forward with a punch at my stomach. I pivoted away and caught his wrist. The force of his blow carried him forward, and I used his momentum to spin him around until I held him at arm's length by the hand and wrist. I increased the pressure gently until he grimaced and tapped his hand against his other leg as a signal of submission. I released his hand, and we bowed to each other.

"You see, an attacker always puts out energy. You just have to get out of the way and then direct that energy. I didn't counter Alex's blow; I just directed his force so it worked against him. Incidentally, if any of you here haven't practiced that throw, it may look like not too much is happening. Let me assure you that that wrist hold is far more powerful than it appears. If you try to struggle or move against it, the pain can be excruciating."

Enough talk, probably too much. I sent them back to practice. One of the kamikazes did seem to be a little softer. Ah, progress.

Alex and his friends were waiting on the mat when my class finished. We bowed to each other, and I waited for the first attack. Alex struck at my head. I stepped away, caught his arm and hurled him forward.

Before I'd completed the throw, his friend moved in with a punch. I spun, caught him and shoved him into Alex who by now was preparing for his second strike. The third man must be behind me. I pivoted just as he struck at my shoulder. My timing was off by a bit, and while the blow missed me, I didn't catch his arm. He recovered quickly and turned on me. Alex circled behind and his friend moved to the side.

I kept moving; they kept attacking. It went fairly smoothly, but my throws didn't always go as well as they should have because I was either too slow or a bit premature. By the time I signaled an end to the practice, I was breathing harder than usual.

As I bowed to Alex and the other two men, I noticed a familiar figure on the bench across the dojo. It was Dan. He'd studied aikido for about a year when we were dating, but he preferred karate and had gone back to it before we were married. I didn't think he was at the dojo to reenlist.

He rose and bowed as I reached him. The rituals of the dojo were so ingrained that they extended even beyond practice.

"Good workout?" he asked.

"Good enough," I answered. I did my best to disguise the fact that I was short of breath.

"Getting in shape for the new case?"

"I try to get in some free-style work regularly, regardless of what I'm working on," I replied. "These days I'm teaching mostly beginners and intermediates, so I need a bit more challenge to keep in shape."

"Don't you ever worry that you'll get hurt if you slip up?" he asked.

"Naw, I love broken bones."

Dan looked exasperated, and I congratulated myself on not letting him suck me into our old battle.

"What brings you to this side of town?" I asked.

"I was over at the Federal Building, and I realized you'd probably be teaching. I heard from Lou Martin this afternoon. He called to ask how reliable you were."

"Did you vouch for me?" I asked, knowing that he had.

"I told him you were my ex, and that, yes, you were completely trustworthy. I did not extend my endorsement to Harman."

It couldn't have been easy for Dan to tell Martin that I was his ex-wife. For Dan, being divorced was already something of a failure; having your ex-wife involved with a smart-mouthed private investigator who was suspected of murder must be painfully embarrassing.

I appreciated his help with Lou Martin, but it didn't really explain his presence at the dojo. To my surprise, I found that I genuinely hoped he'd stay to talk for a while. He showed no inclination to rush off, so I suggested, "I was planning to get a bite to eat at the Vietnamese place near my office. Would you like to join me?"

"Sure," he answered with a smile.

"I'll shower and change and be back in a few minutes," I promised.

Dinner was remarkably relaxed and pleasant, all things considered. We discussed the weather, my beginning class at the dojo, old friends, and his current cases. But through it all, we were both thinking about the Marilyn Wyte killing.

Finally, I said, "Suppose a private citizen gave a police officer information about a crime under investigation by another department. Would he be required to divulge that information?"

Dan smiled, "It would depend on the information. If it was evidence that a private investigator was pursuing and that evidence was not clearly germane to the case, the officer might decide that there was no need to inform the other department."

"That's a lot of words for someone who's usually pretty straightforward. Does it mean that I can tell you what I've learned about Marilyn Wyte, and you won't pass it on to Lou Martin?"

"All those words are supposed to warn you to be careful what you tell me. I can't withhold information that's relevant to a case. I can, however, postpone informing Martin if I know that you'll reveal your findings as soon as they point to a suspect."

"I'd love to tell you what I know and get your reaction to it," I admitted. "If we get to something you'd have to reveal to Martin, will you warn me to stop?"

Dan looked a bit uncomfortable, but it was clear he wanted to hear as much as I wanted to tell him. "I guess I could do that," he responded.

I told Dan what I'd learned from Eileen and from Leo Goldberg. He was as interested in the four mysterious visitors as I'd been. "You have the license numbers; you can get the names from the DMV," he pointed out, waiting for me to ask the obvious favor.

If he'd offered to get the names outright, I'd have accepted gratefully, but the fact that he was making me ask irritated me.

"Yes, I'm planning to get them tonight." I replied, with a certain satisfaction.

"Yourself?" he asked.

"Myself," I responded.

Dan looked stern. "We both know the DMV is closed at night," he said.

"And we both know the DMV computer never closes." I was enjoying this.

Dan cleared his throat and frowned. "Catherine, private citizens cannot just tap into the DMV computer. I know you know that, so I can only assume you have something vaguely illegal in mind."

"I have the access code if that's what you mean."

"Dare I ask how you got it?"

"Is that an official question?"

"God, no. Come on, Catherine, stop playing games with me. I'm off duty. I'm curious, that's all."

"It's simple—and harmless enough. You know the Peninsula is full of computer freaks—brilliant, unorthodox types who get a kick out of beating the system. Jesse's learned all kinds of useful things from them, like how to break into the DMV files."

"Catherine, I don't want to sound avuncular—or worse yet, like a cop—but 'breaking into' the DMV or anyone else's computer could get you in big trouble. More and more sensitive information is stored in computers, and you can bet the people who put it there are going to be very unpleasant to anyone trying to get it out. Why risk it when you can just go down to the DMV tomorrow morning and get the information?"

"Through an official query? Dan, are you forgetting that the DMV notifies owners when a request for information has been made? There's a good chance that one of those license numbers belongs to a killer. Not only would the DMV warn him that he's under investigation, it would have my name and address on file in case he wanted to know who was asking questions. Frankly, whatever the DMV might do to me would be considerably less unpleasant than what this guy would do."

Dan nodded thoughtfully. "I see your point."

"Besides," I said, "if I do it right, I won't get caught."

"How can you be so sure your informants know how to 'do it right'? Jesse's a bright kid, but his information might be out of date."

"Are you offering to run the numbers for me?" I asked.

Dan looked pained. "You set me up for that," he charged.

I smiled. "Not at all. Jesse and I have an appointment to meet at my office at nine tonight to run the numbers. I'm sure he'd prefer to spend the evening with Claire, and frankly I'd enjoy the expression on his face when he finds out I could operate the computer without him. But I wouldn't want you to do something that you weren't comfortable with."

"There was a time you wouldn't have been 'comfortable' with this sort of thing." He said it with an almost wistful tone that softened the accusation. He was right, too. I had changed since I was his wife.

"There *was* a time," I said, smiling. "I'm not quite the good little girl I was then, but I hope we can continue to be friends. I need to get back to the office and set up for Jesse."

"I'll run the numbers for you," Dan capitulated. "But no one—especially your friend Harman—is to know about it. No one!"

My office was up the street from the restaurant, in a stately Victorian whose dignity had been spared the lavish and colorful paint job to which most buildings of its generation were being subjected. It was merely well-kept, not "restored," which meant that it had a comfortable feeling of age and an affordable rent. I was negotiating to buy it, before gentrification reached the block and drove the price out of reach.

My office was on the first floor, with a large bay window, that filled the room with light. I'd put my desk in front of the window, despite Amy's pleas that the area would be perfect for plants. She'd managed to insert a few hanging plants behind the desk, but I drew the line there.

Amy had also lobbied to furnish the room with antiques, but I preferred the simple lines of Scandinavian furniture. The comfortable white leather couch that sat along the right wall wasn't exactly Scandinavian in design but its simple lines fit well with the rest of the decor. The polished wood floor was partially covered by Beluchi tribal rugs in bright red and deep blues. Bookshelves lined the wall opposite the couch, and the computer sat on a small desk against the far wall.

"You'd use that more if you put it on your desk," Dan pointed out.

That was probably true, but I didn't want the computer on my desk. "I don't have room for it there," I said. "Shall I look the other way while you commune with the computer?"

"Hell, no!" he exclaimed. "I'd rather have you learn how to do it right than get directions from some computer freak who might mess up and get you caught. Come on."

The process was reasonably straightforward, though it took awhile. I called Jesse and made coffee while we waited.

When the "Please Wait" prompt was finally replaced with text, we had the names and addresses of three men— Lawrence N. Cannaby, James C. Ralston, and Timothy J. Sutton—and a car-leasing company. I grimaced at the leasing company.

"That one will be hard to trace," Dan commented. "Of course, you could turn it over to the police and let them do it."

"I'll keep that as a fall-back position, but I've got another approach I'd like to try first." This time Dan didn't ask what I had in mind.

Once the computer had printed out the information from the DMV, Dan's reason for staying was gone, but neither of us felt like ending the evening. I poured us a second cup of coffee, and we sat on the couch and discussed the only "safe" subject, the Marilyn Wyte case. The telephone interrupted our conversation.

I picked up the phone. It was Eileen. "Peter's been arrested," she announced.

I restrained myself from using Peter's favorite four-letter word. "Terrific," I said. "Did he call?"

"No, a Nathan Greely called. He's a lawyer."

I knew Nathan Greely by reputation. He wasn't "a" lawyer, he was one of "the" lawyers in San Francisco. "Yes, I know him. What did he say?"

"He said Peter was arrested in Menlo Park late this afternoon. They're holding him in the North County Jail in Palo Alto."

"Go on."

"That's all he said. He left a number for you to call."

I copied down the number and hung up.

"Something wrong?" Dan asked.

"Peter's been arrested."

"That's fast. I'd have expected Harman to be harder to catch."

"So would I," I answered. "I've enjoyed this evening, and I'm sorry to see it end, but I'm going to have to hustle you out now. I need to call Nate Greely."

"Nate Greely . . . Harman does get the high-priced talent," he commented.

"I expect Greely will take it out in trade."

"He'll have to get Harman off first." Dan reached for the doorknob. "Do be careful, Catherine, and please keep in touch."

On that cheery note, he left.

The number Eileen had given me was Greely's home phone number. A woman's voice answered the phone and summoned him.

"Hello." His voice was rich and deep, an excellent voice for a trial lawyer. He was one of San Francisco's small fraternity of superstar lawyers, known as much for his eloquent speeches and occasional courtroom dramatics as for the often sensational cases he took on. In the late sixties he had represented a number of individuals considered subversive and dangerous by the state, but his own lifestyle had remained closer to that of his corporate colleagues than his radical clients.

"Hello, this is Catherine Sayler. I'm calling about Peter Harman."

"Oh yes, H asked me to call and tell you what had happened. He said you were investigating the case with him."

I was startled by Greely's use of Peter's nickname. It was a name he'd picked up in the Haight Ashbury when he was splitting his time between being a graduate student and a member of the counterculture. The only people who used it now were old friends or "street people" from parts of San Francisco and Berkeley that Nate Greely was not likely to frequent.

"I understand Peter's been arrested," I said.

"Around four o'clock this afternoon."

"How'd they catch him?"

"He thinks they were tipped off. They were waiting when he showed up at a little bar in Menlo Park. Even giving the police credit for more investigatory skill than they usually display, it seems unlikely they'd have known exactly where to look for him. Earlier in the day he ran into a fellow who was carrying a grudge; he assumes that's who tipped off the police."

"Who was the guy with the grudge?" I asked.

"His name is Willie Therman," Greely responded. "He used to be a pimp. H tells me Mr. Therman worked the bus station in San Francisco picking up runaways until he picked up a girl from Walnut Creek whose parents cared enough about her to want her back and hired H to help. H has a fairly strong aversion to pimps, and this one made the mistake of getting smart with him. The gentleman ended up with eight stitches in his head and a jail term."

"Any chance the pimp is connected to the people who framed Peter?" I asked.

"H doesn't think so."

"What happens next?" I asked. "Will they set bail?"

"I hope so, though given the seriousness of the crime and the weight of the evidence, there's no guarantee. Even if they do agree to bail, it's likely to be high. I might be able to get them to set it lower if I can bring in enough character witnesses to establish that H is the kind of model citizen who wouldn't be likely to jump bail. Police officers would be the best; can you give me any names?"

"Peter's manner doesn't exactly charm police officers," I said, "but he has a good friend on the Berkeley force, Matt Davis. And there's Hennessy in missing persons here in San Francisco. I'll get his assistant, Eileen, to go through the files and dig out names of officers he's worked with in other cities.

"If it'd help, we can probably also get some fairly powerful people to vouch for him. He's worked for several wealthy families tracing runaway kids. Peter would never ask them to do it himself, but I don't think he'll mind your asking on his behalf.

"That would be very useful. We'll need statements as soon as possible. I could probably find a magistrate who'd agree to a bail hearing over the weekend, but I'd prefer to wait until we can make our strongest case. We can't risk having the judge decide that H is too dangerous to be loosed on the civilian population."

I was actually relieved to hear that Peter wouldn't be released immediately. If the reason for the frame-up was to divert attention from the real killer, Peter had served his purpose and would be far more useful dead than alive. It was possible that jail was the safest place for him at the moment.

"It would be much easier for me to get in to see Peter if I could tell the police I was working for counsel. Would you be willing to certify me as your investigator in the case?"

"I'd be delighted—as long as you don't send me a bill."

I laughed, and agreed not to bill him. We'd settled as much as we could for now, but my curiosity demanded the answer to one more question. "I noticed that you use Peter's nickname. Does that indicate that your relationship goes beyond the purely professional?"

There was a pause. "H was a good friend of my son in college. He helped Jimmy at a time when he needed help that I wasn't able to give. I've always been very grateful. We've worked together enough that I also have a deep respect for him as a professional."

I thanked Greely for his help and bid him good night. I wasn't learning much about who killed Marilyn Wyte, but I kept turning up interesting little bits of Peter's past. I'd have given a lot to be able to go home and snuggle into bed next to his big warm body.

6

I assembled Amy, Eileen, and Jesse at my office earl
the next morning, amid the usual chorus of groans that gree
a Saturday work session. I gave Amy the job of startin
background checks on the three men the DMV computer ha
coughed up. Jesse and Eileen were dispatched to Peter'
office to pull the files of anyone who might vouch for hi
before a judge. I headed for Palo Alto.

I arrived at the North County Jail a little before ten an
asked to arrange a visit with Peter. As soon as I mentione
his name, the jailer stiffened.

"You a relative?" the man behind the desk asked.

"No, I'm a private investigator, and I'm working f
Mr. Harman's lawyer." I removed my license from my purs
and placed it on the counter. The man looked at me, at great
length and more intently than might be considered polit
shrugged, and studied my license. After a period of intens

scrutiny, suggesting either that he was just learning to read or that he was going blind, he looked up.

"Seems to be in order," he admitted regretfully. He continued to stare at me with an insulting smirk.

Ah, a prime specimen of the genus homo chauvinist of the common redneck variety. I led a sheltered life, I realized; most of my contacts were with the white collar set. Their basic attitudes might not be any better, but they'd at least learned to inhibit their more objectionable behavior.

Time for the heavy artillery. I looked at my watch. "It is 9:55," I pointed out. "Visiting hours begin at ten o'clock. I have an appointment with Mr. Harman's attorney, Nathan Greely, at eleven o'clock, and he will be extremely unhappy if I have not seen Mr. Harman by then."

At the mention of Nathan Greely, the jailor became suddenly efficient.

I was shown to a visiting room and told to wait. A few minutes later, Peter strode in wearing a standard issue blue jumpsuit that was cut for someone with narrower shoulders and a bigger belly. The overall effect was considerably less flattering than Peter's usual attire.

"My, aren't you fetching this morning," I said.

Peter grinned at the guard, "Never hire a woman to defend you; they only got one thing on their minds."

He sat down and his expression grew serious as he filled me in on what he'd learned before he was arrested. It wasn't much. No one knew the two thugs who'd held him prisoner and set him up for the murder charge.

"Where does that leave us?" I asked.

"I talked to enough people to be fairly sure that the men I'm looking for aren't Peninsula hires. They're pros—could

be out of town mob, or they could be working for someone
whose business doesn't give them much personal exposure.
Whoever the boss is, he must have plenty of money to hire
those guys, especially if they're on the payroll."

"Clayton's certainly wealthy enough," I confirmed,
"but he may not be the only one with money who was seeing
Marilyn Wyte."

I reviewed what Eileen had told me about the four men
and pointed out that two of the cars were a Mercedes and a
Porsche. "I have the names and addresses of all but one of
the men who visited her regularly," I told him. I did not tell
him that Dan Walker had helped me get them.

"Grady Dawson at Info Search is doing financial background checks on Marilyn Wyte and Hugh Clayton. I gave
him the names Friday morning and told him it was a rush
job. He should have something for us by Monday or Tuesday," I explained. "I'll have him check the financial records
of the other men as well."

Peter chewed on his mustache, a clear signal something
was bothering him.

"What?" I asked.

Peter grimaced. "Grady Dawson's a bit pricy."

"He's not cheap, but he's fast and he's thorough. I
always use him for financial searches. For that matter, his
rates are about the same as mine."

"Yeah, but there's some chance I can get a discount
from you. No way Grady's going to give me one."

"Peter," I said, making no effort to hide my irritation,
"look around you. This is jail, and you are going to be
spending a very long time here unless we manage to prove

that you didn't kill Marilyn Wyte. This is not the time to count your pennies."

Peter chewed on his mustache some more. "Yeah," he said, "it's just that if this goes on very long I'll spend the rest of my life working for Nate Greely."

"That, my dear, is only if you're lucky."

Peter managed a very hollow laugh. "What are you doing about the four guys Eileen gave you?" he asked.

"I think we'll handle most of the background search on them ourselves. Jesse can get Eileen started on a court-record search Monday; then he—"

"Back up a minute," Peter interrupted. "I thought you were finding Eileen a safe place to hide."

"She's staying at my apartment for the time being. She'd like to help with the case, Peter. We can use her for things like the court-record search."

Peter frowned. "I guess it's okay, as long as she stays with records searches. I haven't taught her to do that stuff yet, but she's a fast learner."

"I'll have Jesse handle the other public-records searches, but I'll ask Grady to go after assets and bank records. He's a wizard at that. I'll work on employment profiles."

Peter was chewing his mustache again. "Who's handling interviews?" he asked.

I'd known that question was coming, and I knew Peter wasn't going to like the answer. "Jesse and I."

Peter nodded, but it wasn't a sign of agreement. "I really appreciate all you're doing, but I don't want you doing interviews. Getting information over the phone and searching public records is fine, but I can't have you any more deeply involved. I'll take it from here."

"From here?" I asked sarcastically, indicating the tiny visiting room. "That's going to be quite a trick."

"Nate'll have me out of here in a day or so," Peter responded.

I decided to confront the question of my involvement in the case head-on; he wasn't going let me do it any other way. "Peter, if our roles were reversed, how would you feel if I shut you out, if I refused to let you help me?"

"Dammit, Catherine," he swore, but there was no anger in his voice, "don't do this to me. It'd tear me apart to have you involved in this case. Please, stay out of it."

"I'll stay out if that's what you really want," I assured him. "But it tears me apart to see you in this mess and to be completely helpless. It feels like you don't trust my judgment, like you think you have to take care of me, and you know how I feel about that."

Peter looked hard at me across the table. "I let you help me, and I risk you getting killed. I keep you safe, and I risk losing you another way. It's a hell of a choice."

"But that's what it comes down to, doesn't it?"

Peter looked resigned. "All right," he conceded, "but you've got to realize that you're involved in a different game now. The people you normally deal with are defensive players. They figure out the perfect scam, then when things start to go wrong, they react to what's coming down. The pros play an offensive game. As soon as they realize you're in, they're calculating when and how they'll take you out. You've got to watch your back all the time."

I listened soberly and stifled the momentary fear that he might be right about this case being too tough for me. "What can I say except that I'll be careful."

Peter groaned. "I hope careful is enough. I'm going to be seeing those guys at your door every time I close my eyes."

"Perhaps you should stay at my place when you're out; then you'll be between me and the door," I suggested.

Peter brightened somewhat at the thought and managed a rather anemic grin. "Which reminds me," he said, "how soon is Nate going to get me out of this hole?"

"Monday at the earliest, more likely Tuesday."

Peter groaned.

"He's holding off on the bail hearing until we line up character witnesses to attest to your saintly nature," I explained. "You'll need that if you have any chance of getting out on bail. Besides, jail is not such a bad place for you right now." Before he had a chance to interrupt, I hurried on to explain how from the murderer's point of view it would be highly convenient for Peter to disappear.

Peter snorted, "Catherine, my love, you have the faith of the truly innocent. Only someone who'd never spent time in jail would consider it a safe place. An escape attempt, a fight with another prisoner, maybe a suicide—all very easy to arrange for someone with enough money. If I'm going to be a target, I'd much rather have some space to move. I feel like a fish in a bucket in here."

He was right, of course, and I was chagrined not to have seen the obvious logic of it before. "We'll get you out as soon as possible," I promised. "Eileen and Jesse are rounding up character witnesses, but even with a fistful of statements, the bail is going to be high. Do you need a loan?"

"I make it a policy never to borrow money from a woman, ma'am," he said in a John Wayne voice, then added, more seriously, "I've got some money in the bank, but if it's not enough, I'll take you up on your offer. I appreciate it."

I told Peter about my visit to Leo Goldberg and what I'd learned about Hugh and Susan Clayton. As I'd expected, he was skeptical of the story that she was mentally unstable. "Have you considered that the real target in all this might be you instead of Marilyn Wyte?" I asked.

"You mean that the purpose of the murder was to frame me? I don't think so. Why kill Marilyn Wyte? If the killer was after me, why didn't he choose you? Our relationship isn't exactly a secret. Or why not Eileen? Besides, while I'm not exactly everyone's favorite person, there are very few people I've made angry enough to do something like this.

"However"—he paused as he pulled a sheet of paper from the jumpsuit pocket—"my hosts have provided lots of time for thought, so I've gone back over my checkered past and dredged up the names of the nastiest of my associates. Matt Davis at the Berkeley PD could tell you which of them might be around to cause trouble. He might even be willing to check up on the ones who're on the outside."

I took the list and promised to let Matt handle it. Peter leaned forward. "Now, let's get down to the important stuff. Once I'm out of here, how about meeting me at the Shoals in Santa Cruz?" His grin widened to an unmistakable leer.

"Peter, you're incredible," I exclaimed. "It's a close race between whether you're going to be the murderer's next victim or spend the rest of your life in jail, and you're thinking about sex. This hardly seems the time."

"Even a condemned man gets a final meal."

"Peter, can't you ever be serious?"

"Never more so, my love. There's nothing like eighteen hours in jail on a very solid murder charge to clarify one's priorities." The smile was gone.

There was a lump in my throat, but I forced myself to smile. "Seven o'clock whichever night you get out?" I suggested.

"Good enough." He looked even more serious. "In the meantime, take care. I wouldn't assume that the killer doesn't know you're connected to me, especially after this visit."

"I am always careful. If Nate can't get you out, look for a cake with a file in it."

Peter laughed, though with considerably less gusto than usual.

After leaving Peter, I headed back to the Palo Alto Police Department. I crossed the lobby and strode past the officer in charge with an assurance meant to communicate that I was a frequent visitor. When the sergeant raised an objection, I brushed him aside with a sunny smile and an offhanded, "It's OK, I just stopped by to see Lou," and moved along down the hall before he could respond.

I was in luck. Even though it was a Saturday, Lou Martin was in. He sat in his office, hunched over a mound of papers. His desk was a disorderly assortment of piles of paper, file folders, and stubby pencils. A cup of cold coffee with cream congealing on the top sat forgotten in the midst of the papers. I stuck my head into the doorway and asked almost shyly, "Lieutenant Martin? May I speak with you for a moment?"

Martin looked up with surprise. I found myself looking into those extraordinary eyes that never seemed to smile. I ignored the mild annoyance I could see in his face, and advanced into the room. "Remember me? I'm Catherine Sayler; I came to see you yesterday about the Marilyn Wyte murder."

"Yes? How did you get in here unannounced?" he demanded.

I tried to look surprised. "I just walked in." I paused a moment and smiled apologetically. "I'm sorry, I've been walking into police stations since I was a little girl. Sometimes I forget to go through the formalities. If I'm disturbing you I can come back later."

As I'd hoped, Martin was now regarding me with more curiosity than annoyance.

"My father's a police officer in Denver. And professionally, I've always been in the position of working with the police," I explained. "And I'd like to continue that. We both want to find Marilyn Wyte's murderer. Within certain limits I'm willing to keep you informed of what I learn."

I was standing at a distance from Martin's desk that was socially awkward, calculated to make him uncomfortable without being threatening. He dealt with his discomfort as I'd hoped he would, by motioning me to sit down in the steel chair beside his desk.

"You have something you want to tell me?" he asked.

"I may have something for you, but it's only the loosest kind of hearsay at the moment. I spoke with someone who knew Marilyn Wyte casually, and this person suggested that she expected to come into some money soon."

"Who was the person?" Martin asked dryly. His face betrayed no sign of interest.

I invented a meeting with a fictional lady in a real bar and spliced in a rough approximation of Eileen's conversation with Marilyn.

"You got a name for this woman?"

"I wish I did," I replied, painfully aware of how fishy it sounded. "When I asked for her name, she became very suspicious and wouldn't talk anymore. When I told her I was a private investigator working on the case, she fled like a scared cat. She's not a regular at the bar; nobody knew her name.

"Give me a description." Martin still looked bored.

I gave him a general description of Eileen that could have fit any number of other women as well.

"That description could fit a hundred women," Martin observed, "I'd have expected better from a PI."

I ignored the jibe. "If Marilyn Wyte was involved in something illegal, it might show up in her bank records. I'd sure like to have a look at them."

"Ask Harman's attorney to subpoena them," Martin suggested.

"I can do that, of course. I didn't mean to ask something inappropriate. I'm just used to working with the police. I hadn't realized that wouldn't be possible this time."

I rose to leave, but Martin motioned me back to the chair.

"I suppose I ought to have a look at those records, and it's possible I could let you see them, too. Give me your number, I'll call you."

"Thank you. I really appreciate your help." I handed him my card. He glanced at the card, then at me. "Your father really a cop?"

"He's a captain in the Denver PD." I smiled. "Honest."

I noticed that Martin had not mentioned Dan. I could guess that he shared my father's opinion of my judgment in the matter of men. My parents had been furious when Dan and I were divorced; they were 100 percent on his side. They hadn't met Peter, but I suspected that my dad was probably one of the few people in the world Peter would be unable to charm.

"What's your dad think of you being a private investigator?" Martin asked.

I laughed. "He'd rather I was a nurse or a teacher, but I think he's grateful I didn't decide to be a cop."

"Really. Why?"

"We haven't discussed it much," I explained, "but I think he knows too much about how the men on his force feel about women officers to want me to be one. He didn't have a son, so he raised me more like he would have a boy—gave me his ambition, shared his love of his work— then one day he had to face the fact that there wasn't a place for women in that world. When I became a teenager and still wanted to be a cop, he started telling me it was too dangerous."

"And being a PI is safer?"

"Marginally. Actually, the kind of work I usually do is fairly safe. I deal mainly with white collar crime—it's a better class of criminal."

Martin had relaxed enough to allow his face to show mild interest. He regarded me intently. I wondered if he had a daughter, or if he was simply trying to decide whether I was telling the truth.

"I should be going now," I said. Thank you for your time, and I hope you'll decide to let me see the bank records."

As I left the police department, I reflected that the bank records might well be useless. Marilyn could have kept her money in a secret account or she might not have received it yet. How much money would a woman like Marilyn consider enough to make her rich? And how had she intended to obtain it?

7

I felt tired as I left the police station and realized it must be time for lunch. Marilyn had worked at a company called Microcomp, so I decided to look for a restaurant near there. With luck, I might pick up some local gossip along with lunch.

Microcomp was located in Santa Clara, a couple of towns south of Palo Alto. I suppose you could consider Santa Clara a suburb of San Jose. The two towns sprawl together in the flat basin at the end of the San Francisco Bay, an endless stretch of nondescript houses and industrial parks for "clean" industry.

I located Microcomp in one of the industrial parks. It was a good-sized company, housed in two large, virtually identical buildings. Their stucco walls and tile roofs were what passed for Spanish architecture in California.

A larger street a couple of blocks away offered the usual smorgasbord of fast-food chains. I chose a Denny's. With its orange and yellow plastic decor and predictable sign carved from wonder-wood, bidding me to "Please wait to be seated by the hostess," it could have been in any of a hundred cities across the United States.

But this Denny's was in Santa Clara, and its customers and their conversations could only be from Silicon Valley, that area south of San Francisco dominated by the computer industry. I found myself surrounded by talk of chips identified by four- to six-digit numbers and names of software products that split up words and pasted parts of them back together in a linguistic crazy quilt.

I could hear bits of the conversations on either side of me. The group in the booth ahead was incomprehensible. The two men behind me were at least speaking English. One was obviously trying to get the other to discuss company business that the first man didn't want to talk about.

"What are you guys doing down in that store front in San Jose?" the second man asked.

"You know I can't talk about that. Why the hell do you think they stuck us down there? God, I hate working with Bailey. He's a royal pain in the ass, and I'm stuck with him for at least three months."

"Still, there ought to be a good bonus for working on the superchip."

"Who said it's the superchip?" the first retorted. "For that matter, how do you know the superchip isn't just another company hype? Every time they tighten security, everyone's convinced there's a hot new product coming.

Maybe they just got around to tightening up after that last screw up."

"Naw, that wasn't a big enough theft to have them this nervous. There's too many people working on projects they can't talk about for it to be business as usual. Something's up." At that point the waitress arrived to take my order. I would like to have heard more, especially about the recent theft of chips. From what I was hearing about security in the computer industry, I ought to make Jesse a partner and give him an office down here.

I ordered coffee and a club sandwich, a decision I regretted as soon as they arrived. While the waitress served me, I managed to bring up the murder. "That poor girl who was murdered, didn't she work near here? I don't suppose you knew her?"

The waitress was not talkative. She shook her head. "No, ma'am, will there be anything else?"

I shook my head, and she disappeared. The men behind me were haggling over how to divide up their check, and none of the other conversations around me sounded either interesting or comprehensible.

Time to get down to work. Marilyn Wyte worked for Microcomp. Some of her visitors might be fellow employees. If even one of the men showed up on the Microcomp roster, it would save me considerable time on the background check. It was worth a try, and Microcomp was just around the corner.

I drove the two blocks to Microcomp. The fact that it was a Saturday should work in my favor. I was hoping that a weekend security officer had replaced the regular receptionist. I was in luck.

The security officer was young, in his early twenties at the most; his skin was a chocolate brown, and the hint of a British accent in his speech suggested that he was from the Caribbean. I explained to him that I was trying to locate my best friend from college. I'd lost her phone number, and I couldn't find it in the phone book, I knew she worked for Microcomp, and I wondered if I could take just a peak at the company phone book.

He explained that he wasn't really supposed to do that, but his manner indicated that with a little more encouragement, he would. I smiled and flirted and encouraged him, and he dug out the company phone book.

I started by looking under *C*; my phony friend wasn't there, but Lawrence Cannaby was. "Oh, I forgot, she's separated from her husband; she must be using Sutton, that's her first husband's name." We looked up Sutton, and found Tim Sutton. Two down, one to go. "I just know she works here. Would you mind terribly if we looked up her maiden name? It's Ralston."

There were two James Ralstons, in the book. My three mystery men all worked for Microcomp. I'd hoped for one or two; to find all three was a real break.

I carefully covered my elation with a show of disappointment that my college friend was not in the book, thanked the sympathetic guard, and headed back to my car.

Beyond the fact that all three worked at Microcomp, I didn't know much about the men who visited Marilyn, but I did know their addresses. Sometimes the place a man or woman lives can tell you quite a lot about them; usually their neighbors can tell you even more.

I pulled out a road map and the printout of the addresses from the DMV. The first name was Tim Sutton, and his address was an apartment in Los Gatos. The second was Lawrence Cannaby; his license listed a San Jose address. The third, James Ralston, lived in Palo Alto, and Hugh Clayton's residence was in Woodside. I marked my map with the general area of each of the four addresses. Saturday afternoon was a fine time for a sight-seeing tour.

I decided to start in the south and work my way north toward San Francisco. Lawrence Cannaby's address was in San Jose, so I headed for his place first. I drove through endless developments sprawled over land that once nourished orchards of fruit trees. There were no orchards left and not many trees.

Cannaby's home was in the middle of a small forest of condominiums. I think they call them town houses; they were all attached to one another with identical tiny yards planted with low maintenance greenery.

Cannaby's "house" was one of eight units in a two-story structure covered with redwood shingles. The design of the building was pleasing, and the units had large windows that should have made them wonderfully light inside. It was a nice building but not an expensive neighborhood. If Cannaby was the source of Marilyn's dreams of sudden wealth, he hadn't spent much of his fortune on housing.

Tim Sutton's address was in Los Gatos, a community in the hills that rose behind Santa Clara. Generally speaking, there is a positive correlation between altitude and income in the Bay Area, the higher you go, the more you pay. It's not true for all areas, but it is for Santa Clara and Los Gatos.

Los Gatos is a nice woodsy community, older and
probably stodgier than much of Silicon Valley. Tim Sutton
lived in one of the few apartment complexes in town, a set
of three-story buildings painted light gray with charcoal trim
with a Gothic script sign identifying it as "Oak Manor." I
found the rental office and was greeted by a blond woman
in her thirties who was delighted to describe the benefits of
the Manor.

Security seemed high on the list, though Los Gatos did
not look like a major crime area. She explained with great
pride that the parking area downstairs and the buildings were
"secure." Getting in to talk to Sutton's neighbors was going
to be difficult, if not impossible.

Rents for one-bedroom apartments started at $820 per
month and went up from there. The tenants were professional people, a mixture of singles and couples, no children.
"We are not a swinging singles place," she explained. "Most
of our people work long hours and don't tend to socialize
here much. However, we have excellent facilities for exercise and relaxation."

James Ralston's house was in Palo Alto, the town
Leland Stanford had created for his university when the
nearest existing municipality refused to outlaw the sale of
liquor. Palo Alto broke the altitude-income correlation since
most of the town was on the flatlands, and all of it was
expensive.

Ralston's house was a modern architect-designed
ranch-style affair in a subdivision that tried hard not to look
like one. It hadn't been a cheap development when it was
new, and prices in Palo Alto had escalated in recent years to

put these houses out of reach of all but the affluent. The yards matched the houses, well-kept and expensive-looking, a full-employment program for Japanese gardeners. It seemed like a family neighborhood—a few basketball hoops adorned garage facades—but the bikes and toys that should have testified to the presence of children were missing.

A house across the street and down the block from Ralston's sported a "FOR SALE" sign. I parked in front of it and wrote down the realtor's number. Then I got out and headed for the house next door to it.

A woman in her late thirties answered the door. She was either going out, or people in the neighborhood dressed more formally than they did in my part of the world.

"Excuse me, I'm Caroline Messinger, and my husband and I are considering buying the house next door. I wondered if you could tell me a little about the neighborhood," I said.

She seemed relieved to discover that I wasn't selling magazines or saving souls. "Oh, yes, of course, won't you come in?" she offered.

The amount she knew about her neighbors indicated that "friendly" probably overstated the degree of interaction in the neighborhood. All she could tell me of the Ralstons was that they had young children.

I thanked her for her help and rose to leave. On the way to the door, I asked if there was someone in the neighborhood who'd lived there a long time and knew just about everybody.

"Oh, that'd be Mrs. Moser," she responded. "She lives at 2118 down the block. She knows everything about everybody. But she'll talk your ear off."

Mrs. Moser was obviously the lady to see, and I was in luck—she lived almost directly across the street from the Ralstons. Most neighborhoods had a Mrs. Moser. The uncharitable might refer to her as a gossip or a busybody, but she was also the local historian and the community billboard, providing a kind of social glue. A neighborhood without a Mrs. Moser was a lonely place.

Mrs. Moser was exactly the kind of informant I'd hoped for. I found out about everyone on the block, including the Ralstons. Jim Ralston worked in the computer industry as an engineer of some sort; his wife was a legal secretary who was staying home to raise their three young sons. They were a good Christian family and attended the local Episcopal church each Sunday. Mr. Ralston was a very active in church affairs, he might even be a deacon, though she wasn't sure of that.

It took two cups of coffee and more time than I wanted to spend to get the rundown on the neighborhood, but the background on Ralston was well worth it.

Last stop was Hugh Clayton's address in Woodside. The other three men were merely affluent. Hugh Clayton was rich. His "neighborhood" was an area of small estates, *Architectural Digest* houses set on large grounds, usually with a stable or a tennis court. Clayton's house was barely visible from the main road. It sat at the end of a long drive lined with large oleander bushes, and a metal gate at my end of the drive barred the way.

This was not the sort of neighborhood where one knocked on doors and asked questions, so I headed back for San Francisco.

I arrived home to find LeRoy parked in front of my house. His battered old Ford looked like the tow truck had abandoned it there on the way to the junk yard. He didn't get out, so I walked over to the car.

"Peter says till he gets out, I'm your shadow," LeRoy explained.

There was no point in explaining to LeRoy that I'd managed to take care of myself for thirty-six years and could continue to do so now. If Peter had told him to look out for me, I might as well talk to a door. "All right," I said, resigned to LeRoy's presence on my couch and hoping for Peter's early release, "Come on in."

"I'm fine here," LeRoy responded. "I'll sleep in my car, that way I can watch your house."

"LeRoy," I explained in what I hoped was a patient tone, "people do not sleep in their cars in this neighborhood. The cops will bust you if you stay out here."

"Nope. They won't."

"Trust me, LeRoy. I know this neighborhood. The lady in the white house has probably already called the police."

"It's cool. Lieutenant Walker'll take care of it."

"What," I said, rather louder than I'd intended, "has Dan Walker got to do with this?"

"Mr. Greely called him before he called me. He said he'd tell the uniforms it was cool for me to be here. He's also going to have them keep an eye on your place."

I scowled, and LeRoy grinned. I wasn't sure which was worse—Peter's parking LeRoy out in front of my house or Dan's agreeing to overlook his presence. This was not going to enhance my standing in the neighborhood.

Eileen wasn't in the flat; Jesse was probably still giving her a short course in background searches. I made a cup of tea, changed into my jeans and a comfortable blouse, and got to work on employment profiles.

Most of us love to talk about ourselves and, given the right pretext, will happily supply all kinds of information. The computer industry is young, and there is a good deal of movement between companies. It's the kind of situation where employers actively recruit talent, and headhunters thrive.

Using the British accent I'd perfected for a college production of *My Fair Lady*, I called each of the men and identified myself as representing a placement service that supplied personnel to computer and other high-tech firms. I explained that we were contacting individuals in their areas of expertise to discuss career plans and to offer them the opportunity to submit résumés. The men loosened up considerably when I assured them that all fees were paid by the prospective employers. To my surprise, all three men were only too happy to answer my questions.

Even over the phone they came across as very different individuals. James Ralston was polite and a bit diffident. He responded to my questions but seldom volunteered information. He fit my stereotype of an engineer; he was quiet and a bit formal. Peter would have said "uptight."

Tim Sutton was at the opposite end of the spectrum. While he was only a few years younger than James Ralston, at least a generation seemed to separate them. Sutton was gregarious, talked easily and with great self-assurance. He seemed more like a salesman than an engineer. He assured me that he was always interested in improving his career position. Where the other men identified such factors as intellectual challenge and a degree of professional autonomy as important in the selection of a job, Sutton mentioned only salary and opportunities for promotion.

Lawrence Cannaby was extremely businesslike; he limited the call to fifteen minutes, and while he answered my questions, I could not draw him into a chatty interchange. He was the only one of the three to ask me questions, and his questions indicated a sharp and somewhat suspicious mind. I did not expect him to agree to send a résumé, but he surprised me and promised to put it in the mail on Monday.

I tried to imagine what each of the three looked like. Sutton sounded like the kind of kid who led the pep squad, a big grin and a face that would still look young when his hair began to grey. Cannaby was probably into power lunches and dress for success. He'd looked thirty-five since he graduated from high school. I pictured Ralston as a bit professorial with wire-rimmed glasses and clothes from L.L. Bean.

They wouldn't look as I'd pictured them, of course. But from their houses and their talk, a picture of each of the men was emerging. For shorthand purposes, I dubbed Sutton "the hot shot," Cannaby the "CEO-without-portfolio," and Ralston "the professor."

The personality differences came across more clearly than the differences in their work. I'd asked each man to give me a brief description of his current responsibilities and area of expertise. In each case, the question had triggered a barrage of techno-babble that would have to be translated into plain English before it was of any use at all.

It's patently illegal to tape record conversations without the agreement of both parties, but that didn't stop my trusty Sony from recording all three interviews. Leo Goldberg wouldn't turn me in, and if I was lucky, he'd be the only one who needed to hear the tapes.

I didn't need Leo's translation to get one interesting point. Tim Sutton had made it quite clear that he was currently working on a secret project that could result in "significant advances" in the industry. Thinking back on the conversation I'd overheard in Denny's I wondered if Sutton's project might be related to the "superchip" I'd heard mentioned. It was revealing that while the man in Denny's wouldn't discuss his work even with a co-worker, Sutton volunteered the information that he was working on a secret project. He wasn't the sort of man I'd trust on anything where secrecy was important. If he was working on a secret project, there was little doubt that Marilyn Wyte knew about it.

8

Sunday dawned foggy and cold, a typical San Francisco day. My mood matched the gray sky. I got out of bed, banged my shin on a chair, knocked a glass off the table and broke it, and discovered that there were weevils in the shredded wheat. I wondered what kind of day Peter was having.

Eileen was sensitive to my vile mood and stayed out of the way. I liked that girl better all the time. She rose another notch in my esteem when she brought me a stack of hot French toast, while I sat over the *Chronicle* trying to find the two or three national news stories that I figured must be there someplace.

Jesse called around ten. He'd done all he could on getting together character witnesses for the bail hearing. Now all we could do was wait to see if his efforts would pay off.

I don't normally ask people to work on weekends. I don't usually work on weekends myself, for that matter. But we needed to move as fast as possible. "I'm going down to Palo Alto to interview people in Marilyn Wyte's apartment building. Will you join me?" I asked.

Jesse's response was immediate, bless him—no complaints about Sunday work. He promised to be over in twenty minutes.

I asked Eileen if she had any suggestions for people to interview at the apartment complex. She was not only prepared for my question; she'd drawn a diagram of the place to help us find our way around.

"I doubt that the manager will be much help," she volunteered. "She's spacy and isn't around much. The best person to talk to is Ronald, the maintenance man. He doesn't miss a thing, and he's a lot smarter than he lets on. The upscale set acts like he's invisible." She paused. "He'd probably talk to Jesse more easily than to you."

"Did you ever talk with him about Marilyn?" I asked.

"Not really. I didn't have any reason to. I just started rapping with him because he seemed like a nice guy." She paused. I sensed she had something more to add.

"Something more about the apartment?" I prompted.

"Well, you've probably already thought of this, but I was wondering about the men who visited Marilyn before we started watching her. It might help us figure out what she was up to—you know, prostitution or blackmail or something else. And I think Ronald might know something about that. Like I said, he doesn't miss a thing."

"You don't miss much yourself," I said, and she beamed at the compliment.

Jesse arrived a few minutes later. I walked out to the curb, and after some fast talking convinced LeRoy that Jesse was a sufficiently fierce bodyguard to protect me on the trip to Palo Alto. He headed back to check on his charges at the shelter, and Jesse and I headed for the freeway.

There wasn't much traffic on the freeway on a Sunday morning. Jesse sorted through my stack of tapes, remarked on the fact that I could use a few new ones, and finally pulled a cassette out of his pocket. "Mind if I play one of mine?" he asked.

"Let me guess," I responded. "Tina Turner."

Jesse grimaced. "Bach," he announced. "Flute duets."

"You aren't, by any chance, trying to improve the general level of culture in the office?" I suggested.

He smiled, "It's a dirty job, but somebody's gotta do it."

Marilyn's apartment was in a complex of two- and three-story buildings near the edge of the Stanford campus. Their red tile roofs and sand-colored walls were an obvious attempt to echo the architectural style of their high-toned neighbor. The carefully landscaped complex looked like a nice place to live, but not a cheap one.

The fog of San Francisco hadn't reached Palo Alto, and the day was hot and sunny. Beautiful bodies glistening with oil were artfully arranged around a large pool in the inner coutyard. These sun-worshippers were solid yup—the Chardonnay and brie set, young, thin, and affluent. They were a friendly group, yet none of them knew Marilyn Wyte well. She didn't join in poolside gatherings or even use the sauna or hot tub in the mini gym.

The women around the pool were not secretaries. They were young professionals, and their salaries were considerably higher than Marilyn's had been. The lady obviously had lived beyond her means; I wondered how she'd managed it.

The apartment complex was classy enough to care about its tenants' backgrounds. While Jesse went off in search of Ronald, I headed for the manager's apartment, hoping there might be a file with some information on the dead woman. The manager was in her early forties, too thin by at least fifteen pounds, with a vague look that suggested she was having trouble keeping her attention on our conversation. Eileen had said she was self-absorbed; more likely, she was high.

She expressed horror at her tenant's death but knew no more about Marilyn Wyte than anyone else. I asked if she kept information on her tenants on file and was delighted to discover that she did. She brought me a card Marilyn had filled out. It had just what I was looking for—her home address in Fords Prairie, Washington, and her previous address in San Francisco. It also showed the rent for her apartment. The good life didn't come cheap.

Jesse had found Ronald and their conversation took long enough for me to bask in the sunshine and get thoroughly warm and sleepy. When he finally appeared, the grin he wore suggested that he, too, had learned something. I let him drive back to the city, and on the way he gave me the rundown on Ronald.

"Eileen was right about the dude; he knows more about those people than they know about each other. Didn't have much use for Marilyn Wyte, figured at first that she might be a hooker, but decided later that she was probably just an active amateur. He didn't pay much attention to the men, just noticed there were a lot of them. She played the field, never had only one boyfriend at a time, but most of her relationships were more than one-night stands. The same guy would be around for a month or more, then he'd be gone and she'd take up with some other guy. Ronnie's only been working at the apartment for seven or eight months, but that's been the pattern for the time he's been there."

It was interesting, but I had no idea what it meant. We kicked around what we knew, trying to make some meaning out of it, and finally ended up listening to Jesse's flute duets in silence.

By the time we got back to San Francisco, it was late afternoon. I decided to try Leo Goldberg again. This time he was in. He agreed to listen to the tapes and try to translate into plain English the job descriptions each man had given me. I arranged to drop them off at his office on Monday.

"What do you know about a superchip?" I asked.

"Potato or silicon?" he responded, and dissolved into appreciative laughter at his own joke.

When he'd stopped chuckling, I went on. "I heard some men talking in a Denny's down near Microcomp, and one referred to a top secret project involving a superchip. Do you know anything about it?"

"Catherine, my dear, there is always talk of a superchip or some other top secret project that will lead to a break-through in the industry. Sometimes, there is a secret project that bears fruit, sometimes there is even a breakthrough, but most of the time it's smoke and mirrors, my dear. Smoke and mirrors."

"Meaning, there is no superchip." I said.

"Meaning, there may or may not be a superchip. That term is usually used to refer to microprocessing chips, the little brains of the computers. Everybody's always looking for better brains."

"Would Microcomp be working on a superchip?" I asked.

"I doubt it. I think they deal in random access memory or RAM chips. Do you know what those are?"

For once, I did. Jesse had introduced me to them a few months earlier when he'd decided that the office computer needed more memory. I take his word for such things, but I always like to see what the agency is buying, so he gave me a quick tour of the guts of our friendly PC.

RAM chips look like plastic cockroaches; they're about an inch long and they reside on a very unmaternal-looking slab of plastic called a motherboard. They provide most of the computer's memory; and the more cockroaches you have, the bigger and more complex your programs can be.

"I know a bit about RAM chips," I said. "Could there be a super RAM chip?"

Leo considered my question. "They're always trying to improve random access memory, but the promising areas of research involve developing new types of chips rather than beefing up the existing RAM chips."

"Would a breakthrough be worth a lot of money?"

"Could be. Depends on the breakthrough," Leo replied.

"Would you necessarily know if someone was close to a breakthrough?" I pursued.

"Not necessarily. Companies try to keep that kind of thing secret."

"Do they usually succeed, in keeping a discovery secret, I mean?"

He laughed. "Silicon Valley leaks like a sieve. Big Blue—that's IBM—is about the only one who really succeeds in keeping the lid on. But it's always possible that something's cooking that I don't know about."

"Could you check around for me? I'm particularly interested in whether Microcomp is involved in anything secret. One of the men on the tapes we discussed refers to secret work. Maybe what he said will give you a lead."

"Check around? I'd be delighted," Leo declared with an enthusiasm that set off alarm bells in my head.

"Leo," I cautioned, "take it easy. If there is a secret project, it could very well be connected to Marilyn Wyte's murder. And asking the wrong questions in too obvious a way could be very dangerous."

"Understood," he said in a serious voice. "I will be the soul of discretion."

The words were right, but the tone had an undercurrent of excitement that worried me. I hoped I hadn't made a terrible mistake by getting Leo involved.

I wasn't much in the mood for cooking that night and the state of the kitchen in Ben Lomand didn't inspire confidence in Eileen's culinary skills. I was somewhat ambivalent, therefore, when she offered to fix dinner. But the smells that soon drifted into the living room suggested that I had misjudged her, and dinner confirmed it. She'd stir fried a bunch of vegetables and tossed them over brown rice, and even a confirmed carnivore like myself couldn't help but appreciate the results.

After dinner I built a fire in the fireplace while she made coffee for me and herb tea for herself. Then we settled down in the living room to relax. There was already more color to her face, and her voice sounded fuller, more animated. She was a very pretty girl.

I tried to remember what Peter had told me about her when he hired her. "What made you want to be a private investigator?" I asked.

"Actually, I wanted to be a lawyer, but I don't have the money for law school. I read about a woman in Chicago who went after a slum lord and built a case that got him indicted and forced him to clean up his buildings, and I realized that maybe I wouldn't have to be a lawyer to do something socially useful."

Useful—that was a word Peter used a lot. His definition was a bit more restrictive than Webster's; for him useful meant coercing the haves into tossing a few more crumbs in the direction of the have-nots. It looked like I had another hippie idealist on my hands.

"How did you find your way to Peter?" I asked.

"I met a lawyer who'd worked with Rural Legal Assistance, and he knew Peter."

It figured. The old-boy radical network. Someone was always turning up on Peter's doorstep. But Eileen might actually be quite a find. She was bright, and she might well have the making of a good investigator.

"*Socially useful* isn't a phrase you hear much anymore," I observed, thinking of the Neiman-Marcus set around the pool at Marilyn's apartment complex. "Most kids your age are into success and affluence, things like that."

"Yeah, I guess I'm a throwback. I've always been sorry I missed the sixties. I mean I know it wasn't perfect and a lot of bad things happened with the good, but at least people cared about other people, at least they were trying to make things better."

I nodded. I understood all too well her longing for a world in which social justice was an active goal. Peter was lucky. He'd known the sixties at its best—the idealism, the sense of a community dedicated to building a new and better world. I'd been a bit too young and in the wrong place to find that. Besides, I had another handicap. To people in the movement, the cops and everyone in authority were pigs. To me, those guys in the blue suits were men who'd coached my softball team, bandaged skinned knees, and taken me for ice cream cones. Every time I went home I heard their side of the story—their anger at having their children turn against them, their confusion, their fear. Even now, over ten years later it was still confusing and painful.

I envied Eileen her idealism and wanted to encourage her. Still, there were a few realities about the investigation business that Peter might have failed to point out.

"Doing socially useful work is a fine goal," I said, "but has Peter mentioned the prosaic realities of the light bill and the rent?"

Eileen looked confused.

"Pacific Gas and Electric likes to be paid, so do grocers and landlords. Unless you're independently wealthy, you'll have to earn the money to pay those bills, and socially useful work is seldom lucrative."

"Oh, I realize that," Eileen exclaimed. "Peter does lots of work that's just to pay the bills. I don't expect to save the world. I just want to know that the work I do has some value; that at least some of the time, it helps people."

I couldn't argue with that. The world could use all the Eileen's it could get.

Monday mornings are usually a grim affair. They're either gray which makes me not want to get out of bed, or they're sunny which makes me not want to go to the office. But after accomplishing so little on Sunday, Monday came as a relief. People were finally back in their offices where they could answer our questions or dig out the records we needed.

Eileen was an early riser and fixed breakfast while I showered. I'd miss her company when she went back to living in Berkeley. If someone was watching her apartment, people in the neighborhood should be aware of it by now. Jesse could check the apartment and talk to the neighbors this afternoon, and if all was well, she could return home this evening.

I headed for the office early and was greeted by a wave from LeRoy and a very dirty look from Mrs. Katizakas, who was retrieving her newspaper from the only bush in her tiny front yard. Mrs. K. had once asked what I did for a living, and when I told her she'd looked shocked and asked, "Does your mother know you do that?"

At the office I reviewed the cases we were supposed to be working on and figured out that we could get away with putting them on hold for about a week; after that I could expect several clients to start screaming.

I called my other operative, Chris, who was working on a case in Seattle and briefed her on Peter's situation. She was not enthusiastic about taking time off from her case to drive to Fords Prairie. She was even less pleased when I explained what I wanted her to do there.

"I'm going to be real popular asking questions about a native daughter who was just murdered, especially if they figure out who I'm working for," she complained.

"I have great faith in your natural tact, charm, and ability to lie," I assured her.

"I may also need an ability to run fast."

"That, too," I agreed. "Try to find her best friend, someone she corresponded with after she moved to San Francisco. If her parents aren't helpful, try the high school counselors, her pastor, anyone who'd know who she hung out with. We need to know all we can about what she did after she left home."

Chris grumbled some more, just to discourage me from dumping lousy assignments on her in the future. Being a sympathetic and compassionate boss, I inquired about her current case. She estimated that she'd need at least two more weeks to wrap things up in Seattle. I told her to skip sleeping and do it in a week.

The phone rang at precisely 9:00 A.M. It was Nate Greely informing me that Peter's bail hearing was scheduled for Tuesday morning. I asked about our chances of the judge agreeing to bail.

"Well," Greely said in his sonorous courtroom voice, "this is not the type of case where bail is at all automatic, and H pursues a lifestyle that is not necessarily appreciated by most members of the legal and judicial community.

However, your assistants have come up with a rather impressive group of individuals who are willing to testify that he is just shy of saintly. Since several of those individuals are both wealthy and influential, I think H's prospects are quite good."

I hoped that Greely didn't charge by the word, but it was good to hear that he thought he could get Peter out of jail. The prospect of Peter in my bed was considerably brighter than that of LeRoy at my curb.

Amy and Jesse arrived as I was talking with Greely, and as soon as I finished the conversation, I called everyone into my office. I reviewed the information we had obtained and assigned different aspects of the background searches to Eileen and Jesse.

The address of Marilyn Wyte's apartment in San Francisco might yield someone who knew her, so I sent them there first. The rest of it was pretty straightforward, but the identity of the driver of the leased car remained a problem.

"Maybe they'd just tell us if we asked," Jesse suggested.

"I asked on Saturday, and they won't," I informed him.

"Was worth a try," Jesse said.

I nodded. "Asking was the *A* way; now we try the *B* way." Jesse brightened considerably. I wished that he weren't quite so enthusiastic about slightly shady practices. Peter had once observed that Jesse did a great Eddie Murphy imitation.

"You'll like this, Jesse," I said. "It's almost as good as the stuff they do on TV."

He looked a bit embarrassed, but we both knew he couldn't wait to find out what I had in mind.

"I want you to call the leasing agency this afternoon after three o'clock and tell them you're a writer for a computer magazine. Pick a magazine; it doesn't matter which as long as it's back East so that by 3:30 here, it's 6:30 at the home office. You're doing an article on how computers are used in the car-leasing business, and you'd like to drop by and chat with them about arranging an interview. It'll only take a few minutes. Set it up for today.

"If they'll let you come by, get Amy to make you some phony business cards and go see them. Keep the conversation general, and try to get them to let you see the computer in action. The whole point of the exercise is to get them to show you how the computer works and to get yourself in position close to the keyboard. Then you say something like, 'Let me see if I understand. Now if I typed in a hypothetical license number . . .' and you type in 1DBG835."

Jesse let out a whoop. "All right!" he said. "I like it." Amy suppressed a snicker.

"You're just jealous 'cause I get all the fun," Jesse charged.

"Let's hope it's fun and not a fiasco," I put in. "We don't have a *C* plan."

Jesse nodded. "Yes, ma'am."

9

The one link between Peter and Marilyn Wyte was Hugh Clayton. It was a long shot. After all, Clayton's wife hadn't hired Peter to watch Marilyn. She'd given him a different woman's phone number. But even a long shot was a place to start.

I managed to get Clayton's secretary to give me an appointment for eleven o'clock that morning. I'd have to push the speed limit to make it, but she assured me that it was eleven o'clock today or sometime next week; so I said, "Thank you very much," and headed for my car.

The ever-faithful LeRoy was waiting down the street, and with characteristic reasonableness and flexibility insisted on following me to Palo Alto. I did get him to agree to wait in the parking lot of Clayton Electronics instead of following me inside.

Clayton's office was Peninsula-rich in decor, casual but elegant. The massive wood desk was refinished oak, the floor was covered with a large, expensive oriental carpet, and there were enough plants to decorate a San Francisco fern bar.

Clayton rose as I entered the room. He was a barrel-chested man, about a head taller than I. His reddish beard was touched with strands of gray, and his carefully blow-dried hair gave a hint of thinning at the hair line. He wore a dark gray suit with a thin stripe and a pearl gray silk handkerchief in the pocket.

He smiled broadly and stretched out his hand. "How do you do, Ms. Sayler. What can I do for you?"

I shook his hand. His grasp was firm but gentle; it went well with the oak and ferns.

"I'm investigating the murder of Marilyn Wyte," I explained. "I understand she once worked for you."

The smile dropped from Clayton's face. "Yes, yes, she did. It was an awful thing. But I thought they'd arrested the murderer."

"They have a suspect," I acknowledged. "Would you mind if I asked you a few questions?"

"No, not at all. Are you working for the suspect?" he asked.

"Yes, for his attorney," I replied as I took out a yellow legal pad. "How long did Miss Wyte work for you?"

"About a year. She was a receptionist here."

"I understand she left about a year and a half ago."

"Yes."

I watched Clayton closely for signs of nervousness or stress. There were none. "Can you tell me the reason for her leaving?"

"I believe another firm made her a better offer."

"Did you know her well?" I asked.

"Only casually," he replied.

The lie was delivered with such ease and confidence that it seemed unquestionable. His manner was assured and businesslike, even relaxed. The ability to lie so convincingly did not mean a man was capable of murder; it did make Hugh Clayton a man to watch.

Where do we go from here, I wondered. I decided on a direct tack. Putting down my pad and looking directly at him, I said, "Mr. Clayton, I have reason to believe you're not being completely honest with me."

Clayton looked surprised, but not distressed. "Really, what makes you say that, Ms. Sayler?"

"I know you were seeing Marilyn Wyte regularly before her death."

Clayton sighed and shook his head. "And I thought I'd been so discreet." He still didn't look troubled or upset. "Yes, I was seeing her. I don't know how you found out, but I won't deny it, though obviously I'd prefer that our relationship remain confidential."

"You can count on my discretion if you'll agree to answer my questions."

"Very well."

"Please tell me what you know about Marilyn Wyte. What kind of a person was she?"

"I don't know a lot about her. Our relationship was very intense in some ways and very superficial in others. She was a very beautiful woman, and she was well aware of the impact she had on men. She was always in the present—no talk of the past. I don't even know where she lived before she moved here. I met her at a bar, later I gave her a job. She seemed competent, bright even, but, to be honest, I didn't pay a lot of attention to her job performance."

He was remarkably cooperative for a man in his position—no trace of anger that I'd invaded his private life, no sign of resentment that I represented the man who was accused of killing his mistress. I wondered where he'd learned that kind of emotional control. Maybe they taught it at Harvard Business School.

"Why did she move to Microcomp?" I asked.

"I arranged that. You see, I'm married and even if I weren't, I don't think I'd have married Marilyn. I wanted to end the relationship, and I figured that would be easier if she weren't an employee."

"How did she feel about that?"

"I think she'd have preferred to keep things as they were, but she was smart enough not to ruin what we had by becoming clingy."

"But you didn't end it," I asserted.

Clayton looked down at his hands. "No. I knew I should, but I didn't. I didn't love her, God knows, but I enjoyed being with her, and I missed her. She was . . ." He paused, searching for words. "She was able to make me feel . . . very special—younger, less serious." He paused again, seeming to collect himself, then looked up at me.

"I've told you more about myself than about her, but then I always told her more than she told me."

"Did she see other men that you know of?" I asked.

"Not that I know of, though she may have. She knew it was almost over. She certainly knew I wouldn't marry her, so I wouldn't be surprised if she was looking for another 'sugar daddy'."

"Did you give her presents?" I asked softly, careful not to break the intimate confessional tone the conversation had taken.

"Yes," Clayton sighed. "Of course, gifts are always part of such relationships." Clayton leaned back in his chair and cleared his throat. Turning back to me, he assumed once again the role of self-assured businessman. "Look, I've told you a good deal more than I'd intended. I hope I can rely on your discretion." His tone asserted rather than pleaded.

I nodded and smiled. "Absolutely. I'm sorry to put you through this, but I must know all I can about Marilyn Wyte. Is there anything more you can tell me about her? What kind of things did she enjoy doing? What did she want out of life? Anything that would help me get a sense of her as a person."

Clayton thought for a moment. "I think she was rather ambitious," he said. "She liked nice things, enjoyed the good life. Now that I think about it there must have been another man during the past year or so. I wasn't seeing her that much, and while I gave her some gifts, she didn't get enough from me to keep her in silk blouses and champagne."

He picked up a round glass paperweight from his desk and began playing with it, shifting it from hand to hand as he talked. "I'm making her sound cheap, and she wasn't that way. She was very lovely and vital and alive. She didn't demand gifts, I gave her things because it was so much fun to please her. I doubt that she had to look for another man;

she was the kind of woman who only needs to look available."

"It sounds like her taste ran to wealthy men," I suggested.

"Isn't that true of most women?" he asked with a smile. "I don't mean to be cynical, but given the choice of a man with money or one without, don't most women choose for money?"

"I should think that would depend on the man's other qualities," I said.

"Ah, would that all women were like you, Ms. Sayler, but I suspect that just as men are drawn by beauty, women are drawn by money. But that's no answer to your question. I think Marilyn preferred wealthy men. I can't see her eating in cheap restaurants or going bowling or enjoying the company of men who like such things."

"Was she shopping for a rich husband, or did she just enjoy playing?" I asked.

He shook his head. "I really don't know. If she'd been seriously husband shopping, I don't think she'd have stuck with me for so long. But maybe she didn't worry about that. As I said, she really lived in the moment. I don't think she thought too much about the future."

Clayton seemed to be working awfully hard to convince me—and possibly himself—that Marilyn Wyte wasn't a high-class whore. He put the paperweight back on the desk, and I sensed it signaled the end of our interview. Before he could say anything, I asked, "Since Marilyn worked here for a while, I'd like very much to talk with people who worked with her. I wonder if you'd mind if I spoke with some of your employees this afternoon."

"Not at all. Perhaps you'll find someone who can be of more help than I've been. Nan in Personnel can tell you which of the office staff were here when Marilyn was. She never worked at the plant, so there's not much point in talking to people there. Is there anything else I can do for you?"

"No, thank you. You've been very helpful, and I appreciate your candor."

"I can't see how what I've told you is of much use. But of course, if you think of some way that I can be of further help, please call me. In fact, if you'll give me your card, I'll contact you if I think of anything that might be useful."

I rose and handed Clayton my card. He gazed at me in a considerably less businesslike way, and his parting, "It's been a pleasure to meet you" was spoken with a warmth bordering on the sensual.

Hugh Clayton wouldn't win any popularity contests with feminists, but then he probably didn't care. There were plenty of Helen Gurley Brown fans who'd find him irresistible. There was something about him that reminded me of a randy tomcat that once called my kitchen home. I had the uncomfortable feeling that I might very well hear from Hugh Clayton again.

While he'd tried to conceal his relationship with Marilyn Wyte, he didn't seem overly upset that I knew about it. Blackmail only works on someone who is desperate to keep a secret. Hugh Clayton seemed neither desperate nor particularly secretive.

It was lunchtime, and I found a small Chinese place not too far from Clayton Electronics. The decor was late fifties lunch counter with Chinese lanterns strung around the room. Looked exactly like the Chinese restaurants my parents took me to as a kid. But if the decor hadn't changed, the menu had. No chop suey and chow mein; the cuisine was Mandarin and Szechwan. Whoever said there wasn't progress in the world?

The meal ended with the ubiquitous fortune cookie perched on top of the check. It read, *The meek know secrets the powerful will never learn.* What the hell kind of fortune was that? A simple *You will succeed at all you try* would have been just fine.

The secrets of the meek intrigued me. I wondered what secrets James Ralston was keeping. A fine family man involved with a beautiful woman who ends up murdered— he ought to be both scared and guilty. If I played him right, I might learn a good deal about Marilyn Wyte's relationships with men.

I called Ralston at Microcomp and introduced myself as a free-lance writer. I explained that I wanted to do a story on the problems of balancing family and work concerns, and the minister at his church had suggested that he would be an excellent person to talk to. As I'd hoped, he was flattered and only too willing to grant me an interview. I suggested that I interview him at home, and he invited me to come that evening before dinner.

I called my office and got Amy. Jesse and Eileen were still at the court house searching records and the only message was that Matt Davis had called to say that he had the information on the people Peter had asked about.

Matt was a police officer in Berkeley. He was about ten years younger than Peter, and though he claimed he'd never thrown bricks at police officers or shouted "Pigs" at anyone in uniform, he shared Peter's political attitudes and his basic anarchistic approach to the world. I always wondered how he ended up as a police officer.I dialed the number he'd left. "Hello, Catherine. Sorry to keep you waiting. I don't know if it's good news or bad news, but none of the guys on the list is your killer."

There was a loud crash in the background followed by angry voices. "Never mind the commotion; they're moving some furniture."

I wasn't sure whether that was meant ironically or if the Berkeley Police actually did redecorate their offices periodically. I decided not to ask.

"I checked them all out. Three are dead; three are still in jail, and the fourth has had a religious revelation and is living with a cult in Oregon."

"You're sure the cult member couldn't have engineered the frame-up?" I asked.

"I'm reasonably convinced that his conversion is real. I wouldn't give you odds on how long it will last, but sounds like for the moment he's out of the picture. Anyway, the people in Oregon told me he'd been taking part in a group fasting retreat for the past ten days. They're a weird outfit, but they're not into contract killings."

"Could any of the ones in jail have arranged the killing from there?" I asked.

"Very unlikely," Matt answered. "They're all three loners, not the types to work through anyone else. I think you're going to have to look someplace else for your killer."

I thanked Matt for his help and reminded him of the time of the bail hearing.

By five o'clock I'd talked to everyone who'd known Marilyn Wyte at Clayton Electronics, and I'd gotten the same kind of information I got at her apartment—just about nothing. She hadn't dated anyone there, which was what I'd expected given her relationship with Clayton; and she'd never become friendly with any of the other women.

I called the office again, hoping that someone else had had a better day than I had. I was in luck. Jesse came on the line, full of high spirits.

"I got it," he whooped. "It took a bit of doing, but our mystery man now has a name. The car is leased to a Mr. Burton Monroe. He lists himself as a journalist, and I've already started the background check on him."

"Great work," I said with more enthusiasm than I'd felt all day. "You've got a lot more than I have today."

"And that's not all. I found an ex-wife," he announced gleefully.

"Wonderful. Whose?" I asked.

"Lawrence Cannaby's."

"Do you have anything else on him?" I asked.

"Nothing of any interest. He checks out clean."

"We'll know more about that after we talk to his ex-wife. If Cannaby has a skeleton in his closet, she's the one who's likely to know about it."

Ex-wives were one of the best sources of information around. Friends and coworkers might cover up for you, but ex-wives told all. And the "all" was seldom flattering.

I had one more call to make. I wanted to see if Leo had listened to the tapes of the phone interviews with the three men from Microcomp.

His phone was answered by the departmental secretary who informed me that he was unavailable and asked if there was any message. I gave her my name, and she stopped me. "Oh, Ms. Sayler, just a moment, please. Dr. Goldberg asked me to inform him if you called."

After a brief pause, Leo came on the line, a bit breathless. "Catherine, I'm in a meeting, so I can't talk for long, but I've got something for you."

"From the tapes?" I asked.

"Yes. I think I have some idea what Tim Sutton's secret project involves, and if I'm right, it's worth big money." He paused to catch his breath. "Last time you called you asked about random access memory. Have you ever seen a RAM chip?"

"They look rather like large plastic cockroaches," I replied.

Leo snickered, "Cockroaches, I'll have to remember that. Well, imagine that you could make a RAM chip the size of an ant that was twice as fast and required one-third the crumbs to run."

"Sounds like a better mousetrap," I quipped, shamelessly mixing my metaphors. "Let me make sure I understand what you mean. Are you suggesting that Sutton is working on making a RAM chip that is smaller, faster, and requires less energy than the current chips?"

"That's my guess. He has the right background for it, and it's certainly something Microcomp would like to develop. With a chip like that, they'd have the computer companies lining up at their door. Probably have more orders than they could handle. And the computer applications would be just the beginning. If they could break the size, speed, and power barriers, whole new markets would open up. There'd be microwave ovens, VCRs, calculators, even watches—all the "smart" appliances and gadgets that could be "smarter" if they had more memory. We're talking about the kind of breakthrough that puts a company up in the Fortune 500."

"Can I assume that if someone were willing to sell the design for such a chip, they would find willing buyers."

"You'd have to beat them off with a stick," Leo replied.

I started to thank him, but he interrupted me. "There's one thing more that might interest you," he said. "Lawrence Cannaby has a background very similar to Tim Sutton's and would be a logical member of any team working on this type of chip design. If he's not on the team, it might be interesting to know why not."

It might indeed. I thanked Leo and let him go back to his meeting. I still didn't know who killed Marilyn Wyte, but I had a pretty good idea that it had something to do with Microcomp's secret project.

I arrived at James Ralston's house at a quarter of six. The man who opened the door matched my mental picture of James Ralston—maybe a bit taller, a bit grayer, but pretty much what I'd expected. He looked like the kind of man whose idea of excitement was a well-played game of bridge. This was going to be easy, but I had a hunch I wasn't going to feel very good when it was over.

We chatted casually as he led the way to a small study beyond the living room. The house was decorated with contemporary furniture, probably from a good department store, and fresh flowers from the yard adorned the mantel.

I followed Ralston into the study and stopped just inside the door in surprise. One entire wall of the room was covered with cork board on which were mounted a series of exquisite photographs. Most were in color, though there were a few black and whites. They were studies in form and contour, and it took me a moment to realize that I was looking at close up images of parts of plants and flowers.

Ralston was obviously pleased by my reaction. "You like my work?" he asked.

"It's extraordinary," I replied truthfully. "Both the quality and the composition." The pictures were another side of James Ralston, one that didn't make my job any easier. I liked Ralston. I caught myself hoping that he was not our killer. He was, however, the most likely source of the information I needed, so I forced my mind back to the task at hand and struggled to regain my role of novice reporter.

"One thing I just love about this job is the surprises. I come to interview a computer engineer and discover a photographer." I accepted a seat on the couch. "Of course, the discoveries aren't always good. A couple of days ago I interviewed people who lived near that girl who was killed. You know, the one who was knifed—her name was Marilyn Wyte, I think. She was in the computer industry. Did you know her?"

Ralston was visibly affected by mention of Marilyn Wyte. The casual, relaxed manner with which he'd greeted me disappeared, and he was suddenly ill at ease. But he shook his head and mumbled that no, he hadn't known the girl.

I decided to take a direct approach. "I think you did," I said, fixing my eyes on his.

He crumbled immediately. His face seemed to forget how to hold itself together. The mouth twitched, the eyes widened, and he looked as if he was about to cry. It didn't occur to him to deny the charge. He slumped into a chair and buried his head in his hands.

He was a decent man, and I felt lousy about what I was doing to him. But Peter's life was at stake, so I hardened myself to sound tough. "Mr. Ralston, I'm a private investigator. I already know a good deal about your relationship with Marilyn Wyte, but I need to know more." I went on in a softer tone, "If you didn't kill her and you're willing to help me find out who did, you have nothing to fear from me. No one need know anything about you and Marilyn."

Ralston struggled to pull himself together. Finally, he raised his head. "I don't know anything about it," he said weakly. "I don't know why you're here, but I want you to leave."

"You can talk to me or you can talk to the police," I said. "I can assure you that I'll be a good deal more careful to keep your secret than they will."

He stared at me miserably. I waited; he needed time to assimilate what I'd told him and to reconcile himself to the situation.

I let my voice become gentler. "You weren't the only one, you know. There were others."

He looked startled.

"I know a certain amount about her relationships with them," I lied. "I assume yours was similar."

"I've never done anything like that before. I swear to you; I love my wife and my kids. I don't chase after women."

"No, I'd guess that she chased after you."

He nodded. "Not chased, really, but she flirted. She let me know she liked me. She loved to look at my photographs, and I loved to look at her. She was so beautiful. It was like an adolescent fantasy, and I used as much sense as a horny fifteen-year-old." His voice was bitter.

"But it was more than an affair," I said, letting my voice indicate that I already knew what he was telling me.

Ralston became even more bitter. "She didn't want me, of course. Only a fool would have believed that. She wanted to know about some secret new process." He laughed without mirth. "Well, she missed on that one. She got the wrong man. My one big fling, and it was with a woman who thought I was someone else."

So it had been blackmail, but for something worth far more than a chunk of Ralston's salary—the plans for a new chip-design process. My mind raced, but I carefully kept my excitement from showing on my face. "Why don't we go back to the beginning, and you tell me about it exactly as it happened," I suggested. "When did she start showing interest in you?"

The story was one of a classic entrapment: first the flirting, then a suggestion that they have a drink after work, more drinks, and finally an invitation to her apartment. Marilyn Wyte knew how to make a man feel important and attractive, and for a shy, physically plain man like Ralston, the attention of a beautiful woman had proven irresistible. He'd been a kid in a candy store.

After a couple of weeks of frequent illicit meetings, she had asked about his work, pressing him harder when he didn't want to discuss it. She'd teased him about being a straight arrow, a company man, hinted that smarter, less scrupulous men could turn a position like his into wealth. Finally, ten days before her death, she'd first coaxed, then demanded that he get the plans for the process was working on. She'd threatened to send his wife video tapes of their most intimate moments.

That was the point at which he realized that she had confused him with someone else. His current project had nothing to do with chips and involved a process that was well-known throughout the industry. There was another James Ralston at Microcomp; somehow Marilyn Wyte had mistaken him for the other Ralston.

He'd told her that he was the wrong man; and he'd pleaded and begged. Finally, she'd seemed to believe him, but she had kept the tape and photos in case they might be useful some other time.

"I didn't know whether to be relieved or terrified," he said. "I was still trying to sort it all out when I read she'd been killed. I'd like to say I was sorry for her, but I wasn't. I was just scared to death the police would find the tapes and photos and then the whole thing would come out."

"If the police had the tapes, I think you'd have heard from them by now.

Ralston nodded dully and stared at the floor. "I know how it looks, but I swear I didn't do it. I hated her, and I was scared of what she'd do, but I'm not a murderer."

I believed him. He was the type who might see suicide as a way out, but not murder.

"I don't know who has the tapes," I said, "but if it's not the police, it's almost certainly the murderer."

He looked even more distressed. "If the murderer has them, he probably took everything to destroy it. However, if someone should contact you, I'd like to help."

I handed him my card. "If someone tries to blackmail you, call me at once. If I'm not in, leave a message with my secretary, or if it's after hours, with my answering service. I'll call back as soon as possible."

I tried to make him understand the seriousness of his situation. "Anyone who knows enough to try to blackmail you is involved in the murder, and that means they're very dangerous. You must not try to deal with them alone. Do you understand?"

Ralston nodded. His face was empty of color. He looked dazed. I fought back the pity I felt for him. The worst part was over. Now I needed to help him put himself back together.

I put my hand on his arm. "It's going to be all right," I said. "I'll do everything I can to keep your involvement with Marilyn a secret. In return, I want you to search your memory for anything that might help me track her killer. Will you do that?"

His face had taken on a bit of color, but I could tell by the frightened way he looked at me that he didn't see much difference between me and Marilyn Wyte. "I'll try," he promised.

"Good. I'll call you in a few days, and I'd like to meet you at my office to go over this again. Will you do that?"

He nodded, and we sat in silence for a few moments before he rose to escort me to the front door. "I will call," he said as I left.

I was sorry for Ralston, but it didn't diminish my excitement at the first solid break in the case. Now at least we knew what Marilyn Wyte had been up to. We had a probable motive, and we'd reduced the list of suspects by two. Not a bad day's work after all.

10

Monday night seemed to go on forever. I felt as if someone had left a radio running in my head. I awoke several times to a voice expounding on some aspect of the case. Unfortunately, the voice didn't have anything useful to say, and morning found me tired and unenlightened.

A night like that was a sure sign that I was using my head too much and my body too little. I forced myself to climb out of bed and put on my running clothes. If I couldn't get to the dojo, at least I could run. I was out the door and down the street before I was fully awake, which is the only way I can manage to run in the morning. If I take time to think about it, it doesn't happen.

I don't really like to run. It feels good for a few minutes, then it starts to hurt. Peter was a great runner and always claimed that if I ran more, I'd get past the point where it hurt.

But I'd watched him run, and I knew that you don't get past the hurting, it just takes longer to get there.

As I woke up, I became aware that LeRoy was following me in his mobile junk heap. The perfect complement to a less-than-perfect morning. I ran as far as I could without getting sick, then walked home.

I was glad I'd sent Eileen back to her apartment the night before. I was in no mood for company. I showered, dumped some tea and cereal into my grumbling stomach, and headed for the office. I'd hoped that my morning run would make me feel better; it had only given me a better reason to be tired. The one bright spot in the day was that I managed to convince LeRoy to go to the bail hearing. Peter wasn't the only one who was going to feel claustrophobic if he didn't get out of jail soon.

Tim Sutton's résumé had arrived in the afternoon mail Monday, but Cannaby's and Ralston's weren't there, and it might be days before they came. I decided to see what I could get from the personnel department at Microcomp. I wasn't optimistic. Personnel officers tend to take the right to privacy very seriously.

I called Microcomp and explained that I was conducting a background check for a client and needed some information on the work records of several of their employees. The personnel director was a woman, brusque and busy and not too long on phone manners. She finally agreed to grant me a few moments of her time that morning.

I called Tim Sutton's previous employer, a company called Electricorp. It was a small firm, and when I asked for the personnel department, I was referred to the CEO. He was a genial, rather talkative man who took considerably longer than I'd expected to comment on his previous employee. Sutton had come to him about seven years ago, and had worked there for ten months.

"He'd only had one job before this one," the executive informed me, "but he had an excellent college record and a good recommendation. He knew stuff that guys five years his senior don't usually know. A real sharp kid."

I asked about the reason Sutton had left.

"Money," he replied. "I knew right away I couldn't keep a kid like that for long. I was surprised he even took the job in the first place. We're a little firm, and we can't pay anything like the big guys. A kid like Tim can make two or three times what I can afford to pay him."

"Do you know anything about his previous employer?" I asked.

"Little firm back East, as I recall," he said. "I talked to his previous boss on the phone; he gave Tim a real good recommendation. I don't remember the name of the company, but if it's important, I can probably find it in my files."

I checked Sutton's résumé. "Was it Upland Electronics in Cambridge, Massachusetts?" I asked.

"Could be. I really don't remember. It wasn't a big-name company; don't think I'd heard of it before."

I thanked him. It was noon back in Massachusetts, no point in calling Sutton's previous employer now.

I arrived a bit before 11:00 at Microcomp, and was escorted to the personnel department. The personnel director, Ms. Lisa Canelli, was a tall woman in her late twenties. She wore a dark blue pin-striped suit and white blouse that would have fit right in at IBM. Her expression matched her clothes, very businesslike, but her manner was brittle. Only the insecure work that hard at being professional.

Her youth and probable lack of experience could be advantageous. Instead of trying to cajole her into giving me what I needed, I decided to act as if it were standard procedure for the personnel department to cooperate with an external investigator.

I explained that the names of three employees of Microcomp had come up in the course of an investigation, and I needed to check on some information. I wound up with the assurance that I would, of course, maintain the rules of confidentiality standard in such cases.

My speculations about her proved to be correct. She hadn't encountered a situation like this before and was unwilling to reveal her lack of experience. After a moment's hesitation, she followed my lead and asked exactly what type of assistance I required.

"I'll need to review the personnel files of the three men," I replied. I reached into my purse, "Of course, you'll need my license before you can release them to me," I added, placing the license on her desk.

It would never have worked with someone who knew more about the business. The license meant nothing more than that I'd passed a multiple choice test and worked for another investigator for three years. It was certainly no proof of honesty or integrity, nor a free pass to browse through personnel files. But I had ignorance and vanity on my side, and the efficient Ms. Canelli hurried off to get the files. Had I been doing my usual kind of job, I would have plugged this leak instead of pumping it.

She came back with the three files, looking increasingly uncomfortable. "Exactly what information do you need?" she asked.

"Just the usual sort of thing," I replied, "past employment record, character references, work evaluations." I was really pushing it by asking for so much, but the worst she could do was throw me out, and a look at that much material was well worth the risk.

"Well, I'll have to review them first to make sure they don't contain any sensitive material," she asserted.

"Of course. I can work in here if you prefer, though I should think it would be more convenient for you if I worked in another office."

She leafed through the files, and pulled some papers from the third one.

I raised an eyebrow and tried to bend my face into a question mark. I must have gotten close, since she looked a bit ruffled and explained, "This individual is working on a project of some sensitivity." She extended the files and offered to show me to a meeting room where I could look through them.

Ms. Canelli had only removed papers from one file. That meant Cannaby was not included on the special project team with Tim Sutton. I hoped his folder would tell me why. Toward the back of the folder I found a sheet with the notation, "Interviewed for Alice team, rejected because unwilling to commit to substantial overtime at present."

Alice? Alice who or what? Alice Walker, Alice B. Toklas, Alice's Restaurant, Alice in Wonderland? A line from the Jefferson Airplane played in the back of my mind. "One pill makes you larger, and one pill makes you small."

Alice could be the code name for a new design process that would result in a smaller, more powerful chip. It could also be the code for a new brownie, but I was betting on the chip.

Why would Lawrence Cannaby refuse a spot on what must be a prestigious research team? I wondered if Marilyn Wyte had something to do with his reason for not wanting to work overtime.

I checked all three folders for former employers and the personal recommendations. Beyond that, what I read gave me some sense of the three men but not much more.

Cannaby was praised for his dedication and hard work, his attention to detail and precision, and his willingness to work overtime when a project required it. Ralston was lauded for similar virtues. Both men were good team workers and showed leadership potential. Cannaby's refusal to work overtime on the Alice project just didn't fit with the other information in his folder.

Sutton's file was the one from which Ms. Canelli had removed papers; his statements about working on a secret project had not been an idle boast. He got high marks for creativity and ingenuity. Two supervisors noted that he was quick to grasp a point and was a first-rate problem solver. No one praised him as a team player, but there were no complaints about him either. I came across a single letter dated two years ago from a supervisor complaining that Sutton was taking too many sick days and might have a drinking problem. Nothing indicated that he had been treated for alcoholism. Ms. Canelli had been thorough; there was no reference to Alice or any other secret project.

I compared the men's employment records. Sutton had worked for three companies in ten years. Ralston had been at Microcomp for ten years and had worked for only one other company before that. Cannaby was a mover. He'd worked a number of places, usually for two to four years. Each move had involved a substantial salary increase, with one exception. He'd come to Microcomp from a firm called Ares Technology, leaving there after only six months and moving to Microcomp for slightly less than he'd been making previously. I circled Ares Technology on my pad and made sure I'd copied the address and phone number correctly.

All three men made salaries in the $40,000 to $60,000 range.

I spent as long as I dared with the files. Even my gullible friend would get suspicious if I took too long. It took some effort to restrain my enthusiasm as I thanked her. It wouldn't do to look too pleased.

I'd made it to lunch without obsessing about what was happening at Peter's bail hearing, but my stomach was jumpy as I dialed the office to see if Amy had word of the outcome. She had, and it was good. Peter was a free man, temporarily. He'd asked Jesse to remind me of our appointment that evening.

It was just after noon; figuring an hour an a half to get to Santa Cruz, that still left more than five hours of working time. You could get a lot done in five hours. Some of it might even be useful.

I still had to canvass Cannaby's neighborhood as I'd done Ralston's, a less-than-thrilling prospect because I didn't expect to get much information this time. Ralston lived in a residential area where people tended to know each other. Cannaby's condo was in a neighborhood of upscale singles and professional couples who spent considerably less time at home and were less likely to know their neighbors. I'd be lucky just to find someone home on a weekday afternoon.

Keith used to say that detective work was ninety percent tedium and ten percent excitement. Ten percent was probably an overly generous estimate. I resigned myself to an afternoon of tedium, had a quick lunch, and headed for Lawrence Cannaby's neighborhood.

There weren't many people home, and only one of them knew Cannaby. That was a woman down the block who complained bitterly that he had been rude and belligerent when she quite accidentally put a small dent and several scratches on his silver BMW. My brush with the Buy America Brigade gave me a lot of sympathy for irate automobile owners. Cannaby'd get no black marks from me on that one.

I dug into my purse and found the slip of paper on which Jesse had written the number of Cannaby's ex-wife. She worked at a medical research firm in Santa Clara; I called, hoping I could meet with her during her coffee break. Her reaction to the information that I was calling about her ex-husband was irritation. "I haven't much to say on that subject," she announced in a voice that said just the opposite.

She finally agreed to see me but with a noticeable lack of enthusiasm.

The ex-Mrs. Cannaby turned out to be a tall, very slender woman with features so fine they seemed hard.

There was a tightness about her—in her voice, the way she stood, the way the skin seemed pulled a bit too tight across her cheekbones. Beneath her white lab coat she wore a bright red jumpsuit, numerous gold chains, and suede boots.

Her answers were short and didn't tell me any more than I'd asked. She was the kind of interviewee who made you work for everything you got.

I was getting to the hard questions. I'd hoped the preliminaries would loosen her up, establish some rapport to make the hard part easier. No sign of loosening or rapport, but I plunged on anyway. "Was your ex-husband promiscuous?" I asked.

She gave a snort. "Larry, fool around? I doubt it. Not that I'd care. He wasn't that great in the sack. I can't see him running after women; he was never overly interested in sex at home." She dug around in her purse, fished out a cigarette, and lit it, then remembered to offer me one. I shook my head.

She was loosening up. The cigarette was part of it. I waited for her to go on.

"No, Larry was no Casanova—too damn busy. Other men might come home, have a drink, and get romantic. Larry'd bolt down dinner and head for his lab in the garage, and I wouldn't see him till around eleven. Unless, of course, it was Friday or Tuesday—then I'd see him at ten, like punching a time clock."

"So he was very involved with his work," I prompted.

"Oh God, yes. And that was about all he was involved in."

"Was he ever involved in anything illegal, as far as you know?"

"No, he barely drinks, and I don't think he's even tried coke. He's a model citizen."

"Is he capable of violence? Could he, under any circumstances, commit murder?" That question always got their attention.

The answer was not what I'd expected. "He'd kill his own grandmother to make it big in the industry," she declared bitterly. "Larry's one vice is ambition," she explained. "His brother is a very successful businessman. He has his own company, and Larry's dad is always bragging about how much money his younger son makes. Drives Larry crazy. That's what he was doing all those nights in the garage, working on schemes that were going to make him rich. Money isn't enough either; he wants to be famous, a kind of second generation Steve Jobs or Adam Osborne."

"And you think he'd kill to achieve that goal," I suggested.

"Well, that's a bit strong," she said in retreat. "I don't suppose he'd actually kill anyone, but I wouldn't guarantee his honesty if a little dirty work would do the trick."

"Do you know anything about what he's working on now?" I asked.

She shook her head. "No, I don't see him often, and after years of putting up with his obsession with technology, I tune out whenever he gets on that subject."

We talked a bit more, then it was time for her to go back to work. As she left, she said, "I didn't really mean he'd kill someone. Larry's a schmuck. He has the emotional maturity of a two-year-old, but he's not a killer."

That, I thought, is what they all say.

* * * *

There wasn't any point in visiting Sutton's apartment house. The woman in the rental office had made it clear that she didn't allow nonresidents inside the complex. Besides, her description of the tenants suggested that they'd know little about each other and tell even less. I remembered the reference to alcoholism by Sutton's supervisor and decided to check out the bars. There were three in Los Gatos—two upscale places and one of the dark and smoky variety that catered to good ol' boys. In addition, there were several restaurants that had their own bars.

I wandered into one of the upscale bars and ordered a scotch and water. I hate the taste of scotch, which makes it a perfect drink for those occasions when I want the appearance of drinking without the results.

As the bartender left my drink, I said shyly, "Uh, I'm looking for an old friend, a guy I worked with. He used to live around here. His name is Tim, Tim Sutton. He's about six foot, brown hair, dark eyes." I paused and tried to look both embarrassed and eager. "I wondered if maybe he came in here. See I'd like to meet him, but I'd feel weird calling. I thought if maybe I just bumped into him . . ."

The bartender smiled. I had the feeling he might have heard the story before. "Used to be a guy like that named Tim who came in here, but he hasn't been around for over six months. And I don't know his last name, so I can't tell if he's the one you want."

"Oh," I said, having no difficulty looking disappointed. "You might try Spades," he offered. "If it's the same guy, he liked to play the ponies; and Spades is a good place to meet people who play the ponies."

I thanked him enthusiastically and asked directions. The bar was several miles down the road, and I had just enough time for one more visit before I headed off to see Peter.

Spades was your basic bar, definitely not an upscale place, no ferns and brass for these folks. A long bar extended down the length of one side and tables were arranged along the other. Pictures of horses and jockeys covered the walls. It wasn't the sort of place single women went to alone, but it was late-afternoon happy hour, and the regulars at the bar looked curious rather than menacing, so I plunged on in.

My discomfort made it even easier to play the role I'd fashioned for myself, and when the bartender delivered my scotch and water I launched into the routine I'd used in the previous bar. If anything, I was more convincing this time, but the bartender's response bordered on hostility.

"Don't know any Tim," he said, and moved on down the bar.

He'd told me what he wanted me to know, and he wasn't going to tell me any more, so I took a drink of the scotch and retreated out the door.

The bartender followed me to the door, glowering all the way. He either hated women or knew Tim Sutton and for some reason didn't like questions about him. I hoped it was the latter.

11

The Shoals in Santa Cruz was a lovely Victorian mansion on the finger of land that formed the Northern boundary of Monterey Bay. It was a classic California bed and breakfast with a paint job that probably cost more than the original price of the house. Its blue-gray walls were accented with shades of mauve and purple, and carefully tended beds of flowers matched the house's color scheme.

I climbed the stairs and rang the bell. A young man I hadn't met before greeted me. When I told him I was meeting Peter Harman, he smiled broadly and a bit conspiratorially, "Ah, yes, the cupola room. If you'll just follow me."

"I know the way, thank you," I said. "Is Mr. Harman here yet?"

"He certainly is."

I climbed the stairs to the cupola room. It was the smallest but the nicest room in the Shoals. The room itself was circular, with windows on all sides. You could stand on one side and look out at the ocean, then turn and see the coast range through the opposite window.

I knocked, and Peter called, "It's open."

He was sitting on the window seat facing the bay, and to my surprise, he was wearing a suit. Peter never wore suits. In the year we'd gone together, the most formal attire he'd worn was a sports coat and slacks. Yet here he was in a charcoal pinstripe suit that looked like it had been made for him. It certainly hadn't come off the rack.

I was so surprised that I just stood and stared. He was obviously delighted by my reaction. "You like it?" he asked. "Like it" was an understatement. The dark jacket emphasized the width of his shoulders and the trousers narrowed his hips. He looked at once sexy and elegant. "It's certainly better than the last thing I saw you in," I answered, determined not to fall all over myself just because he was wearing a suit. "Where did it come from? You didn't just pick it off a rack this afternoon."

"No, Nate Greely bought it for me several months ago when he wanted me to testify at a trial. He took one look at my sports coat and told me to go get a decent suit. He wanted me to look like a lawyer or stockbroker."

"Well, it does that," I agreed. "It is actually very flattering. Why did you wait so long to wear it?"

"General cussedness, I guess," he replied as he crossed the room. "You can be so spit and polish proper, I was afraid that if I started wearing a suit you'd want me to do it all the time."

"I'm not all spit-and-polish proper, Peter," I said. "And much as I like the way you look in that suit, it still doesn't compare with how good you look without it."

Peter let out a hearty laugh and swept me into his arms for a long hug. A firm pressure against my stomach suggested that I shouldn't plan on dinner too soon.

"You're glad to see me," I said.

"I never could keep anything from you," he laughed.

"You men are so transparent."

"We all have our crosses to bear."

"Don't you want to know what I've found out about the murder?" I asked.

"Only if you've figured out how to save my hide. Otherwise, I can wait." He was already deftly unzipping the back of my dress.

I'd taken out a few minutes to purchase a little surprise of my own. Peter expressed his appreciation with a whistle as my dress slipped to the floor. "Very nice," he said, "Lace and satin become you, milady."

I'd expected our lovemaking to have a rushed, even desperate quality under the circumstances, but if Peter felt any desperation, he certainly kept it well hidden. He made love with his usual gusto, and as usual I had to submerge my concern about the neighbors.

Afterward, I lay beneath him feeling the pleasant weight of his body on mine, our breathing falling into a shared rhythm. It was unthinkable that anything should separate us. Peter's breathing deepened, and his body grew heavier, a sure sign he was slipping into sleep. "Hey, big fella, time to roll over before you squash me," I whispered in his ear. He gave me a sleepy kiss and obligingly rolled off. I snuggled against his body.

A few minutes later, he asked lazily, "Do you always sleep with your clients?"

"Only the big, good-looking ones, but in your case I made an exception."

He chuckled. "How about another exception?"

We ate on the pier. There were places with better food in town, but Peter wanted to look out over the water. He stared at the sea as he'd been doing when I arrived at the Shoals. Finally, he said, "It's very healing, isn't it?"

I nodded, and he continued. "All that sky and water, there's something comforting in the vastness of it. The night John Kennedy was shot and I thought the world had gone crazy, I drove out to the beach at San Gregorio and spent most of the night looking up at the sky. It was so black you couldn't see the ocean, only the white of the foam as the waves crested and broke. There'd be a flash of white and it would shoot along the wave line, then die as the water washed up on the beach."

He was silent for a moment, then the waitress arrived with our orders. Peter's plate was covered with something that appeared to be large spiders and rubber bands dipped in batter and deep fried.

"Calamari," he said. "Want some?"

"No," I said firmly. Squid was not one of my favorite foods.

"Want to tell me what you've found out?" he asked as he speared one of the rubber bands and put it in his mouth.

I gave him a brief summary of the information we'd collected. He was particularly interested in Ralston's story and the reference to the Alice project in Cannaby's file. The other bits and pieces didn't add up to much, but there were some interesting possibilities. "I thought you might want to hang out at Spades a bit," I suggested.

He nodded. "Just my thing," he said. "You sure you won't try this? It's delicious." He extended one of the spiders toward me, with a twinkle in his eye that told me he knew very well that I did not want anything to do with his dinner.

I shook my head. "I try not to eat eight-legged creatures," I said.

Our banter hid the subject I'd been avoiding, my role in the investigation. Peter had been very clear about his desire that I not be involved. I didn't expect that he'd changed his mind. Now that he was out of jail, he'd want to run things, and I had a feeling that I'd end up sitting behind a desk if he had his way.

"Where do we go from here?" I asked.

"You mean with the investigation? What you're already doing seems right, as long as you and Jesse can afford the time. I'll check out Spades, and I want to work with a sketch artist to try to work up a picture of the two goons. Once we have a picture, I can send it to people in Vegas and some other places. Right now it's just a matter of following all the trails till one of them leads somewhere. More wine?"

I was too busy being amazed to answer, but he filled my glass anyway.

"Something wrong?" he asked.

"No, not at all. I was afraid you wouldn't want me to continue working on the case, now that you're out of jail."

"I don't, but we settled that at the jail," he said simply. "You were very clear about how you felt. I have to respect that. I don't have to like it, but I will respect it. We're both too damned independent to let the other call the shots, but so far we've been pretty good at working together."

I raised my glass, "To working together then."

He touched my glass and grinned lecherously, "Very closely," he added.

"How'd the bail hearing go?" I asked.

Peter laughed. "It was downright embarrassing. I spent most of the time trying to figure out who the hell they were talking about, sure didn't sound like anyone I know."

"Jesse said he thought they were nominating you for sainthood."

"That's better than LeRoy's analysis. He figures they were practicing their eulogies."

I got to the office late the next morning but in a much better mood than I'd been in all week.

"Hugh Clayton called," Amy informed me as I walked in the door.

"Well, well, well," I said, as she raised an eyebrow. "Any message?"

"Just to call him."

I took the message slip with his phone number and went into my office. Mr. Clayton was on another line, but his conversation conveniently ended when I gave his secretary my name.

"Catherine! Thanks for returning my call."

"What can I do for you?" I asked.

"I'm going to be in the city this evening. I was hoping you'd agree to join me for dinner."

Dinner. So I had read his warm parting correctly. Never pass up a chance to get to know a suspect, I thought as I informed him that I'd love to dine with him.

"Good. I'll pick you up at seven," he replied. "What's your address?"

I wasn't about to give my home address to anyone connected with the case. "I'll be working late. You can pick me up at my office." I gave him directions.

Amy and Eileen were waiting expectantly when I emerged from my office. "A dinner invitation," I said. "Tonight."

Amy raised her eyebrow again; Eileen looked concerned. "Clayton could be the murderer."

"Could be," I agreed. "But he's not likely to do me in over dinner."

"You seem awfully sure of that," Eileen said.

I was. Our killer was a cautious man, a planner. If he decided to go after me, he wouldn't make an appointment.

Jesse came in about half an hour later. He looked excited. "I think we got a live one," he said. "Burton Monroe doesn't check out right. I think he's a spook."

"What have you got?" I asked.

Jesse perched on the edge of the chair and pulled out his notebook. "Monroe lists his profession as journalist, but his employer is an obscure Japanese trade publication. He's got an expensive house, membership in a couple of exclusive clubs, and owns an airplane. He's either independently wealthy, or he's got another source of income.

"I know a reporter from the *San Jose Mercury,* so I called and asked about Monroe. He knows him, says he's always at every press briefing and full of questions. Affable guy who loves to take people out for a drink and a chat. No one knows where he gets his money, but there are those who suspect he traffics in information—in short, a spook."

"Spying for the Japanese?" I suggested.

"Or anybody else with the cash, I expect," Jesse replied.

He was grinning broadly, and he had reason. I wondered how long it would be before one of my clients had the good sense to hire him away from me.

"I'll call Peter," I said. "Tell Eileen we'll meet here in about half an hour."

Peter came straight over. We assembled in my office and Jesse repeated his report. "Sounds like a spook all right," Peter said. "Damn good work, Jesse."

"If you're right, Monroe would have the connections to line up the two goons who grabbed you and not too many scruples about how to get rid of a would-be blackmailer," I said. "Where do we go from here?"

Before he could answer, Amy came on the intercom. "The packet from Grady Dawson just arrived."

"Bring it in," I urged, feeling like it was Christmas morning.

I was even more excited as I scanned Grady's report. In five neat piles I had the financial information on the four original suspects and the victim. Grady had put a big red star on the top of Tim Sutton's and Hugh Clayton's files. I glanced at Clayton's.

The information that Grady had been able to get about Hugh Clayton's financial situation was clearly incomplete. Grady was a pro, and it took a very fancy bookkeeper to get by him. Clayton looked like a man with something to hide.

I handed the Clayton file to Peter and turned to the one on Tim Sutton. A quick look at the file told me why Grady had starred it.

We had the first of the month figures for his bank account, and Sutton's balance went up and down like a yo-yo. Some months he had a huge balance; others he was broke. It was a good bet he was a compulsive gambler, and the size of his occasional wins suggested that he wasn't placing his bets with a small-time operator.

Across the bottom of the sheet, Grady had written, "No records for subject prior to 1978; no accounts in Boston or Cambridge. Do you want us to pursue this further?"

Peter was busy reading the file on Hugh Clayton. I shoved Sutton's file across the desk to him and reached for my own folder on Tim Sutton. Both the résumé he'd sent me and the employment record he'd submitted to Microcomp named Upland Electronics as his employer in Boston. I dialed the number he'd given for Upland.

After a few moments of transcontinental static, a woman's voice answered, "Upland Electronics."

I asked to speak to the personnel department, and she explained that they were in a meeting at this time and asked if she could take a message and have them return my call. Something in the well-rehearsed, almost toneless way she said it made me suspicious. "Is this the Upland office or an answering service?" I asked.

"This is their answering service," she replied.

I declined to leave a message, and hung up with a sense of excitement.

"There is no Upland Electronics," I announced. "And I'd bet that there is no Tim Sutton. For some reason, our Mr. Sutton changed his identity seven years ago."

Peter whistled. "We've got quite a set of suspects. A spook, a gambler without a past, a wealthy businessman whose financial records elude even Grady Dawson, and an ambitious engineer! A lively group."

"I'd prefer one with a shady record and three sterling citizens. It'd make matters a lot easier," I commented.

"Do we have anything more on why our ambitious engineer wouldn't work overtime on the secret project?" Jesse asked.

I shook my head. "From his ex-wife's description, he doesn't sound like a man who'd let passion get in the way of ambition. I'd like to know more about what he's doing in his garage-laboratory. If he's onto something important on his own, that would explain his reluctance to give the company any extra time."

"It might also explain Marilyn's interest in him," Peter remarked. "If she thought he might be the valley's next multimillionaire, she'd have happily invested some time in getting close to him."

We needed to know more about Cannaby and his research. "I think Jesse and I should arrange to chat with Cannaby's coworkers. Maybe one of them knows something."

"Maybe," Peter said, "but I don't think it's a high priority. Don't forget that our killer must have underworld connections of some sort. You don't hire thugs from Manpower."

My stomach rumbled indecorously, reminding me that it was past lunchtime. "Anyone hungry for lunch?" I asked. Everyone was.

I called Amy in for sandwich orders. By the time Jesse and Peter finished suggesting little extras to make the meal more interesting, it looked more like a banquet than a working meeting.

"Your neck is practically in the noose, and you're thinking about your stomach," I charged as Peter called Amy back to order baklava.

"Life's too short not to get the most from it, Catherine," he replied. "Enjoying my lunch isn't going to make me work any less hard."

"That's what I get for working with a hippie," I grumbled. "Amy, bring a baklava for me, too."

We passed around the files from Grady and exchanged the information we'd collected. The last three files provided no surprises. Ralston and Cannaby lived on their salaries; Marilyn Wyte lived considerably beyond hers.

We'd all reported on our findings except Eileen. Her work had been fairly routine, and I didn't expect any great revelations, but I wanted her to feel a part of the team. "Do you have anything we should know about?" I asked.

She shook her head. "The routine record searches haven't turned up anything," she reported. "I interviewed the manager at the place Marilyn gave as her former address. It's a nice, fairly expensive apartment house. The manager says he doesn't even remember her, but I'm not sure I buy

that. Men don't easily forget a woman like Marilyn." She
paused. "It bothers me how no one seems to know much
about this woman. She doesn't seem to have connected with
anyone, made any friendships or stirred any animosities. I'd
like to go back to the San Francisco apartment and interview
the tenants. Maybe I can find someone who knew something
about her."

"Sounds like a good idea," I responded. I was pleased
to see her curiosity overcoming her fear. She could have
stayed safely in the office and waited for us to tell her what
to do, but she had chosen to become an active part of the
team. I was glad I'd agreed to let her work on the case.

"There's one thing I don't understand," Eileen said.

"What?" I asked.

"I can see Ralston as a blackmail victim. He's a family
man. But what would Sutton or Cannaby have to lose?"

"A blackmailer specializes in secrets," I said. "There
are plenty of things people don't want exposed besides their
sex lives."

While we were trying to eat our baklava without getting
honey and nuts all over the table, I suggested that we each
rank the five men from the most to least likely murderer.
Everyone put Ralston at the bottom of the list. Cannaby and
Clayton ranked as possible but not likely. We hadn't come
up with a motive for either of them, but there were too many
unanswered questions about Cannaby, and Clayton had
gone to too much trouble to hide his assets to be completely
honest. Sutton and Monroe tied for most likely murderer
with two votes each.

"Grady wants to know if we want him to keep digging
into Clayton's finances," I told Peter. "Do we?"

Peter shook his head. "Clayton's no fool. If he doesn't want anybody to know about his finances, it could take Grady months to unravel them. We don't have the time, and I don't have the money."

"I have a dinner engagement with Hugh Clayton tonight," I announced. Peter grimaced but said nothing.

"It'll be interesting to see if he tries to pump me for information. I doubt that his motives are purely social, but we'll see tonight."

"I'll check out Monroe," Peter suggested. "We'll need to know more about him, and I know some folks on the Peninsula who may be able to help. If he turns out to be what I think he is, LeRoy and I may pay him a visit."

I didn't like that idea much, but if I didn't want Peter looking over my shoulder, I had to extend the same courtesy to him.

That left Sutton, and the story of his past was in Cambridge. The phone calls to Upland Electronics had to be referred to someone, and I wanted to talk with that person.

"Two down, one to go," I announced. "If I take the 'red-eye special' out tonight, I can be in Boston tomorrow morning." Peter frowned. "You going alone?"

"It seems like a one-person job," I responded. "You three have plenty to do here."

"I don't like the idea of you being there without any backup," Peter complained.

"I can use the Boston Police for backup if things get tight. They're good at that."

Peter looked unconvinced.

"Besides, either Sutton is innocent, and I have nothing to worry about, or he's guilty but he's across the continent. Either way, it's not terribly risky."

"Wrong. A case like this is risky all the way along the line. At least three of these guys are probably crooks, and as soon as they realize we're asking questions, we could have all three on our tails. Sutton or whoever he is may have been into some serious stuff. His buddies could be hoods or junkies. They won't like you asking questions."

I nodded grimly. He was right, dammit.

"What does it take to change identities?" I asked.

"A fake birth certificate at the very least. Maybe some other papers," Peter answered.

"Not the sort of thing you buy at the corner drugstore."

"Hardly. It takes money and connections to get fake papers. There've been enough spy novels with detailed descriptions of how to set up an identity that I suppose you could try a do-it-yourself job, but most people who need new identities are already on the shady side of the law and know where to find the experts."

"Meaning that if Sutton isn't Sutton, he probably has underground connections in Cambridge or Boston," I said.

"It's a fair guess."

"Okay," I said. "I'll take it slow and easy and check on who I'm seeing before I go calling. If it looks at all dicey, I'll call Amy and arrange a regular phone check in."

Peter shook his head. "There's a better way. I know a PI in Boston you can call if you need someone to watch your back. He's a real character, a bit macho, but someone you can trust. He can also help you with information on the underworld."

He fished in his jacket pocket for his notebook. "If he asks who the hell Peter Harman is, tell him I'm the hippie radical he almost got killed looking for the Simon kid." He copied a name and phone number on a piece of paper and handed it to me.

"Is this a first name or a last?" I asked.

Peter shrugged. "He never said."

I stuck the card in my purse, hoping I wouldn't need to use it.

12

Tim Sutton had gone to a lot of work to hide his former identity. When I finally tracked down the person who was taking his calls, I'd need a good story to convince him to even talk to me. I spent the next couple of hours playing with different possibilities. After trying a number of farfetched ideas, each with a potential flaw that could get me killed, I finally concocted a scheme that seemed workable. As I figured out the details, I was filled with a heady sense of elation, followed shortly by the sober realization that I was beginning to enjoy this sort of thing.

I'd spent a good part of the last few days inventing stories and pretending to be someone I wasn't; the uncharitable name for all that was *lying*. I had to admit that after years of working scrupulously and carefully "by the book," I enjoyed breaking my own rules. Dan was right; I had changed.

A glance at my watch reminded me that meditations on the future would have to wait. I called Amy in and asked her to create a bogus letter of introduction. "Do we still have stationery with the Masters, Kilbrune, and Colby letterhead?" I asked. She looked confused. "That's the fake legal firm we created for a case a couple of years ago," I reminded her.

"I think so," she responded, "Let me check."

The letterhead was buried in the bottom of a closet that only Amy dared to enter. Finding it took longer than typing the letter.

Chris called from Seattle around 4:30. Getting information in Fords Prairie had been easier than she'd expected. There were plenty of townspeople who were quite willing to talk about Marilyn Wyte. She was considered more of a black sheep than a native daughter.

"Marilyn was a mediocre student with a reputation for being fast," she reported. "In her senior year of high school she got pregnant by the scion of a wealthy family in Olympia, but he bought his way out by paying for the abortion instead of marrying her. Her family's working class Baptist; they wouldn't see me, but other people from their church were quick to denounce Marilyn's wild ways."

"Anything about what she did in San Francisco?" I asked.

"That's harder," Chris replied. "But let me do this chronologically. After high school, she went to junior college for a year, then dropped out. Her family sent her to secretarial school in Seattle. Washington was too dull for her, so she went to San Francisco to look for a job. That's where things get fuzzy.

"I found one old friend who stayed in touch with her, but the friend claims not to know much about San Francisco. Marilyn lived there for five years before she moved to Palo Alto. The first year she worked as a secretary, but she quit that job, and her friend doesn't know what she did after that."

I sat up straighter in my chair. "Did they lose touch, or did Marilyn refuse to tell her what she was doing?" I asked.

"The friend says Marilyn just never said much about her job. I think the girl is lying. She knows what Marilyn did, but she doesn't want to tell."

Chris' devotion to chronology drove me crazy. It always meant the important stuff came at the end, when I was nearly asleep. But she was a good investigator, and her sense of people was excellent.

"I think Marilyn was a call girl," Chris announced. "Or she was involved in something else she couldn't talk about that paid big money. Everyone mentioned that she had a lot of money after she went to San Francisco. Came home wearing fancy clothes, driving a nice car, and bringing expensive gifts."

So Marilyn's enjoyment of the good life had begun before her meeting with Hugh Clayton and her arrival in Palo Alto. It figured. She could have been a call girl, or she could have been the mistress of someone like Clayton. Whatever she did, it almost certainly involved sex and money, a combination that might well have led to murder.

I slipped out for long enough to throw a few clothes in a suitcase and dress for dinner. I pulled on a silk dress that was sufficiently dressy for dinner with Hugh Clayton and durable and comfortable enough to survive the flight to Boston. Then I hurried back to the office to wait for Clayton.

He arrived at 7:00 sharp.

"So this is what the office of a real detective looks like," he commented, looking around the entry hall. "I notice that in novels, the detectives' offices are always on the upper floors of seedy buildings, while on television, they seem to be in fancy skyscrapers. This is much nicer than either."

"Are you a mystery fan?" I asked, more to make conversation than anything else.

"Only on airplane flights," he replied. "I fly quite a bit, and they make better reading than company reports."

He took me to dinner at the Carnelian Room, atop the Bank of America Building. I loathe the building; it rises like a heavy dark monolith out of the sparkling whiteness of the rest of the city, looks awful up close and worse from far away. The big advantage of eating there is that it's one of the few places you can get a view of the city without the B of A in it. When it came to ordering Clayton played the patriarch and suggested items for my approval. "Do you like pate? Good, we'll start with the duck pate with pistachios." He surveyed the wine list and sent the waiter off to find a bottle that didn't appear on the list but that he was sure the steward stocked. I was reminded of Peter's third law—people who know too much about wine usually know too little about anything worth discussing.

I waited for Clayton to ask me about the case, but he didn't. He made small talk. It was looking like an evening of good wine and poor conversation, but when I asked about his business, I got a pleasant surprise. He chatted easily about it, full of information and funny anecdotes.

Over the veal piccata, which was a bit heavy on the lemon and light on the capers, he exclaimed, "Well, I've told you about what I do. Now it's your turn. What's it like to be a private investigator?"

"Much less glamorous than either the books or movies," I replied. "It's mostly asking questions and gathering information."

"I suppose everyone asks you this, but what made you decide to become a private investigator?" he asked.

He was right; everyone did ask, usually with the unstated suggestion that it was not a suitable occupation for a woman. Clayton seemed to read my thoughts. He laughed disarmingly and said, "That must have sounded terribly sexist; it's just that women don't often choose professions that involve a good deal of danger. I'm curious what attracted you to it."

"Not the danger, certainly," I replied. "In fact, my job really entails very little danger. I don't normally accept cases involving criminal violence. I work in corporate security."

"Which is?" he asked.

"Which is helping someone like you find out who's talking too freely to the competition or helping himself to company profits. That sort of thing. White-collar crime."

"And that's not dangerous?"

"White collar criminals are seldom violent," I said, not mentioning the mild-mannered accountant who turned out to be an ex-Green Beret and tried to slice me up with his letter opener. "No high-speed auto chases, no hanging out in dark alleys, no gunplay. It's mostly going over the books and asking questions. All very civilized."

"But Marilyn Wyte's killer is most certainly violent. Doesn't that worry you?" He seemed more curious than concerned.

"I sincerely hope never to meet Marilyn Wyte's killer," I replied. "My job is gathering information."

Clayton looked skeptical. "It seems to me that the more successful you are at that, the more danger you're in." He paused and looked slightly embarrassed. "I'm afraid my male chauvinism is showing. I catch myself wanting to warn you that this case is too dangerous for a woman. Perhaps it bothers you less than it does me. I'm quite unnerved whenever I think of what happened to Marilyn. I wouldn't want to get anywhere near the person who did it."

He refilled our wine glasses, and I realized that the bottle was empty. I'd been so entertained by Clayton's stories of the computer industry that I'd drunk more than I intended. Maybe it would help me sleep on the plane.

"On a less macabre topic, tell me more about your work. How does one get to be an investigator? Do you take courses in college or apprentice yourself? How does it work?"

"It's mostly a matter of apprenticeship of one kind or another. The state requires that you spend three years working under professional supervision, so unless you're a former police officer or have worked for the FBI or Treasury, you start out working for another investigator."

"Earn while you learn, an old and honorable institution."

"Except that you don't earn much for the first couple of years, but I suppose that's always been true for apprentices."

"Indeed, in the middle ages they were lucky to get their supper and a drafty attic to sleep in."

My salary for the first year with Keith hadn't bought much more than supper and a tiny studio apartment, but if he'd been tight with his money, he was generous in many more important ways. "There have been some improvements," I admitted.

Clayton continued to ask questions about investigative work, and to my surprise they were intelligent questions—not the usual "tell me about your most exciting case" questions but more thoughtful ones about practice and ethics. His curiosity and desire to understand more than the superficial level of the job were evident. I was enjoying myself thoroughly when I realized that the combination of his skillful inquiries and a very fine Pinot Noir had conspired to make me more talkative than I intended. Leo was right about Clayton's talent for getting people to talk. I'd assumed that he must be manipulative, probing for the information he wanted. Instead, I found him simply curious, a man who seemed to enjoy knowledge for its own sake.

The waiter came for our dessert order. I was about to pass when Clayton took over and ordered a raspberry tart for me. "They're too good to miss," he assured me. Our conversation had made me more favorably disposed to him, but he ruined that over dessert. The waiter had no more than poured our coffee and discreetly disappeared than Clayton was angling to get me back to the apartment he kept in the city. I'd told him I had to be back at the office by 10:30 to make a call to a colleague in Saudi Arabia. Now he suggested that he could wait while I called, then we could go back to his place for a nightcap. He seemed incapable of believing that I did not want to go to bed with him. Pressed for a reason, I announced that I did not sleep with married men.

He chuckled condescendingly over my Victorian morality, but he stopped pressing so hard. I managed to get back to the office without a wrestling match, for which I was profoundly grateful—since I'd have been sorely tempted to break his arm.

Like Penelope's shroud, the San Francisco International Airport is perpetually under construction. It took me fifteen minutes of wandering around the latest set of detours to find the long-term parking area but I made my plane with twenty minutes to spare. I grabbed a pillow and blanket, and slid into my seat. As the flight attendant explained how to transform the seat cushion into a flotation device, my thoughts drifted to my dinner with Clayton.

Clayton hadn't tried to pump me for information on the Wyte case. He had asked a lot of questions about my work. Could have been sizing me up, I suppose. I'd talked freely, but I'd carefully avoided letting him know I could defend myself. The less said about that the better.

White-collar criminals weren't as docile as I'd led Clayton to believe. There'd been several times I'd had to ward off an attack. The ex-Green Beret was the only one who was a real threat: that escapade had cost me my marriage.

It had been a fairly routine case until I confronted the accountant with the information that I knew he was embezzling funds. He should have buried his face in his hands and issued an anguished confession. Instead, he reached in his desk and pulled out a letter opener with s six-inch blade. I knew from the way he handled it that he wasn't your usual accountant, but it was only later that I found out he'd been trained in hand-to-hand combat by the Green Berets.

I'd managed to disarm and subdue him without getting so much as a scratch, but when I proudly related my exploits to my husband the cop, instead of congratulating me on my prowess, he issued an ultimatum that I had to get out of the detective business. His claim that my work was too dangerous didn't square with the fact that it was the Green Beret who'd wound up in the Emergency Room; and since I was the winner, I didn't appreciate the suggestion that I was "damn lucky" to be alive. Instead of drinking champagne, I ended up sleeping on the couch in my office, coming to grips with the fact that loving someone didn't mean you could live with him.

Airplanes are not made for sleeping, especially when they stop along the way so that one set of groggy people can climb off and another set can climb on. I awoke with the stewardess asking if I was ready for breakfast. My mouth was fuzzy, and my eyes felt like the lids were lined with sandpaper. My stomach was jumpy, and my neck cracked when I turned my head. I was too old for the red eye special.

The plane arrived at 10:46 A.M. It was really 7:46 San Francisco time, but my body felt like it was 3:00 A.M. There was no way on earth that I was going to get back on that airplane without a good night's sleep. I called the Parker House and reserved a room for that night.

A quick check of the mirror in the restroom revealed that my clothes looked better than I did. No need to change and thus no excuse for a shower.

I headed for the car rental booth. I wanted something big enough to afford some protection from Massachusetts drivers and small enough to fit into the parking place I would never find. I needn't have bothered. They only had a few choices anyway, and I ended up with a Chevrolet slightly larger than a tin can and not nearly as sturdy.

I found the answering service by 1:00, but the door was locked, and it was 1:45 before the girl who ran the office wandered in. She was obviously the secretary rather than the manager. She was in her twenties, and she'd have been much prettier without all the makeup. She wore a tight knit dress and very high heels.

I had no legal standing in Massachusetts, which was only a little less than I had in San Francisco. But I figured she wouldn't know that. I flashed my license and explained that I wanted to see the file on Upland Electronics. She shook her head and said that she didn't think she could give it to me. I explained the seriousness of the situation, that this was a murder investigation and the court could subpoena the records. I used lots of big words. She wasn't impressed.

She sat and chewed her gum for a few minutes, checked her fingernails, and finally replied, "I could, like, get in trouble, you know. I mean I'm not supposed to give out information and stuff." She paused and checked her nails again, then looked at me sharply. "On the TV sometimes when people want information, don't they, like, pay for it?"

I don't generally pay for information; I don't even have any idea of the going rates. I flashed back to my first sortie into the adult world of dining out and the agonizing problem of what was a proper tip. The girl was watching me shrewdly. I'd damn well better look like the detectives on TV, or I was in trouble.

I nodded and opened my purse and pulled out two twenties and laid them on the desk without speaking. She looked at the money but didn't reach for it. "It's not very much," she said, sounding disappointed.

I pulled out another twenty and put it on top of the others. "That's what it's worth to me not to have to get a subpoena," I announced, "no more."

She picked up the bills and went to the filing cabinet to get the Upland file. It gave me what I wanted—the name of the person to whom messages were forwarded, his phone number, and his address.

I copied the information and returned the file the girl. "Address an envelope to yourself," I instructed her.

"Why?" she asked suspiciously.

I took another twenty out of my wallet and held it where she could see it. "Because I don't want anyone, especially anyone from Upland Electronics, to know we've had this discussion. If you are able to keep a secret, I'll send you this. Do you understand?"

She looked impressed. I guess I had finally managed to behave like a real private eye.

The name in the Upland folder was Alexander Brody. The address was in Chelsea. My Massachusetts geography was a bit rusty. I hoped Chelsea was where I thought it was, close to Boston, and not off at the other end of the state.

It took two gas stations before I found a map. To my relief, I found Chelsea just north of Boston, across the Mystic River. It wasn't a long drive, once I figured out how to get on the freeway and over the Tobin Bridge.

I took the Chelsea offramp and drove through the downtown. The main street was lined with small stores that looked like they'd been around for a long time. Woolworth's was the class act on the block. It all seemed very gray.

The buildings on Brody's street were all brick; decades of industrial grime had dulled them to a gritty somber rust that even the bright autumn sunshine couldn't lighten. Brody's apartment was one of six in a three-story brick building in the middle of the block. Like its neighbors, it had seen better days. My eyes were drawn to a movement in the window of the ground-floor apartment on the right side of the building. The window was partially covered by a sheer white curtain that hung from above and ended about two thirds of the way down in a wide border of lace. On the window sill, a menagerie of porcelain animals turned their backs on the sidewalk. I'd found my neighborhood informant.

I rang the bell. She'd already seen me, of course. It took her only a moment to get to the door, but unfastening the multitude of locks took longer. There must have been at least four, each with its own metallic tone. A symphony of security.

She was a large, plain woman with an Irish name and the hint of an accent. She'd raised her children in this neighborhood and hadn't lost the habit of being concerned about her neighbors.

Alexander Brody had lived upstairs from her for eight years. She described him as a "nice young man," not wild or loud, and a good tenant. He was unmarried and didn't seem to have many friends. He didn't sound like an underworld character, but then what did I know about underworld characters?

I had a couple of hours before Brody would be home from work. Chelsea wasn't the sort of city that offered tempting ways to kill time, so I decided to pay a visit to the *Boston Globe*. Sutton had changed his identity seven years ago; I had a hunch it had to do with some crime. If the crime was a big one, it might have been in the *Globe*.

The trip to the *Globe* offered plenty of opportunity to reflect on the difference between Massachusetts and California drivers. In California the prime rule of survival is "Go with the flow." That's what makes it possible to have four lanes of traffic, bumper to bumper, driving sixty miles an hour. Everyone just plugs into the flow of traffic and acts like they're part of a single stream.

In Massachusetts, there is no stream. There is a deadly collection of aggressive individualists, all switching lanes and cutting in front of each other constantly. I felt like I was in the midst of a giant game of vehicular tag.

I managed somehow to make it to the *Globe* building in one piece. As I got out of my car, I had a deep appreciation for how Columbus must have felt when he finally stepped ashore on land. I hoped I hadn't risked my life in vain.

I found my way to the newspaper library only to be told that the files were not open to private citizens. The librarian, a nice looking young man in his late twenties, offered to find the information I needed.

"I'm afraid I don't have a date or a very specific description of the event." I explained. "I'm looking for all crimes involving companies connected with the computer industry during 1978. It's the kind of thing you'd have to search through the whole year's papers to get." He seemed nice, but no one is *that* nice.

"It might take an hour or so. Is that all right?" he asked.

He smiled broadly when he saw my astonishment. "We have everything on computer," he announced proudly. "I put in a couple of key words, and the computer does the rest. In less than an hour, you'll have every story on computer-related crimes during 1978. Of course, you'll only get stories that were printed in the *Globe*," he explained with the patient condescension of a kid elucidating the operation of a new electronic toy to an elderly relative.

It took forty-seven minutes to be exact, during which time I made the awful mistake of accepting the offer of a cup of coffee. My stomach complained loudly for the next two hours.

There were five stories of computer-related crime in 1978, not exactly a crime wave, but four were similar enough to suggest a gang operation. That possibility hadn't escaped the police; in the story on the fourth robbery, an inspector mentioned that the crimes might be connected.

I asked for printouts of the five stories and left with the coffee slowly eating away the lining of my stomach. There was no way of knowing which, if any, of the crimes Sutton was connected with. I hoped that Alexander Brody might help with that.

13

I drove back to Alexander Brody's neighborhood and parked across the street from his building. The yellowed shade that covered his front window was illuminated from within. My stomach felt like a washing machine during the agitation cycle. I couldn't tell if it was my nerves or the *Globe's* coffee. I figured I might as well get the interview over with, so I locked the car and headed for Brody's apartment. A man in his mid-thirties answered the door. He was wearing faded jeans, a V-necked sweater over a white T-shirt, and running shoes without socks. He was Mr. Average—average height, average weight, average looks; he would have disappeared in a half-empty room. He stared at me blankly with a slightly pained expression on his face. I'd probably arrived in the middle of a ball game.

"Alexander Brody?" I asked.

He nodded. "Yeah?"

"I'm Catherine Sayler. I represent Masters, Kilbrune, and Colby. I'm here about the will."

"What will?" Brody asked.

"You have heard from Mr. Colby, haven't you?" I asked. "He was supposed to call you, to notify you of the inheritance. Oh dear, you haven't heard from him." I bit my lip and continued. "Could I come inside, please? I have some bad news, I'm afraid."

Brody stepped back. "Yes, of course, come on in."

The apartment was average, too — somewhere between neat and messy. The newspaper lay on the floor near the couch, and the end tables were covered with a variety of objects that hadn't found their way back to the kitchen or bedroom. The furniture was from his parents' basement or Goodwill. A yuppie he was not, and if he had any connection to organized crime, he was definitely at the low end of the salary scale.

Brody offered me a seat on the couch, and I took it, fidgeting and doing my best to look uncomfortable. I waited while he sat down across from me. "Mr. Colby was supposed to tell you," I repeated. "I'm afraid that a friend of yours is dead, Mr. Tim Sutton."

It took Brody a moment to recognize the name. His first reaction was shock, followed quickly by suspicion.

"Oh, I know his real name wasn't Sutton, though that's the name he used in the will. He left you a sizable portion of his estate; Mr. Colby was supposed to explain that, too."

Brody reacted to the mention of an estate and an inheritance as I'd hoped he would, with considerable interest. "Who is Mr. Colby? And what's sizable?" he asked.

I handed him the letter Amy had typed on the Masters, Kilbrune, and Colby stationery. It introduced me as a representative of the law firm and explained that I was conducting an investigation connected with the will of a Timothy J. Sutton of Los Gatos, California. I gave him a few moments to read the letter, then answered his second question, "I believe that your share of the estate is roughly $125,000."

Brody looked dazed. "I . . . $125,000?"

"Roughly," I replied. "However, there are some problems with the will that we were hoping you could help us with. As you know, your friend did not make the will in his legal name. Now there's no law against changing your name, but it can make matters more difficult when it comes to probating the estate."

I went on to explain that it was important to provide the judge with clear and thorough answers to any questions that might arise in order to avoid a lengthy court proceeding. "If the judge decides to question the validity of the will, he could hold up the distribution of the inheritance for years; and of course, then there would be court costs that would be paid out of the estate before you received your money."

Brody ran his hand over his hair several times. "What do you need from me?" he asked guardedly.

"The most important thing is Mr. Sutton's real name. It would help to have a date and place of birth so we could obtain a birth certificate."

Brody seemed to relax a bit. I'd have loved to know what he was afraid I was going to ask. "His real name was Timothy Stratton," he said, "and I think he was born in Lawrence. His birthday was April 12, two days after my sister's, but I'm not sure of the year. Probably 1950 or '51."

I pulled a yellow legal pad from my briefcase and wrote down the information. "Is that Lawrence, Kansas?" I asked.

"No, Lawrence, Massachusetts, up north of here. We grew up there. I can't believe he's dead. What'd he die of?"

"There was an automobile accident," I said. "There were no witnesses, so no one knows exactly what happened. The police are treating it as an accident, though for some reason they haven't officially ruled out foul play."

"What's that mean?" he asked. "That they haven't ruled out foul play?"

"*Foul play* means that someone caused the accident, that it was murder. But I don't want to worry you; it probably doesn't mean anything in your friend's case."

Brody sat silently for a moment. Then he ran his hand over his hair a couple more times.

"I'm sorry to be the one to have to tell you, and I'm even sorrier to be asking questions at a time like this. But of course, it's in everyone's interest to get the will probated quickly."

He nodded, and I continued. "Is there anything we should know before we take the will to a judge? I mean, well, when a man changes his name without a clear reason, sometimes the court gets suspicious."

Brody looked troubled. Something, perhaps commitment to his friend, warred with his desire for the money. Greed won out quickly enough. He leaned forward and looked down at the floor as he talked.

"Tim got in some trouble here, and he figured he'd never get a decent job if people knew about it. He was very bright—like, maybe he was a genius. He was the brightest kid in our graduating class." Brody paused and looked up at me. It seemed important to him that I realize that his friend was exceptional. It occurred to me that being a friend of the brilliant Tim Stratton might have been one of Alexander Brody's major achievements.

"He really loved computers," Brody continued. "After college he got a job with a computer company, a really good job. He was making big bucks, doing real well. But he got mixed up with the wrong people. He let them talk him into helping them boost some chips. The cops caught the guys red-handed. They couldn't prove Tim was the inside man, but everyone knew it, and he lost his job."

"I see," I nodded sympathetically. "How tragic for someone so gifted."

"Yeah, it was." Brody began picking at a loose thread on his sweater. He was completely oblivious to the small hole that his nervous habit was producing. "Tim wasn't really a bad guy. He'd never have done something like that on his own, but he'd gotten into gambling, and he owed these guys a lot of money. That's why he did it, to get out from under."

"So they caught everyone but him."

"Not everyone, just the punks who boosted the stuff. The punks stonewalled and so did Tim, so they never got the guys who set the whole thing up." Brody twisted the thread between his fingers, and the hole in the sweater slowly grew in size. "I think the reason they came down so heavy on Tim was he wouldn't talk. His boss told him they'd make sure he never got a job in the industry again. That's why he had to move and change his name."

"He must have done very well in California," I commented, "to have left such a large estate."

"Yeah," Brody responded. "He said he was doing good, but he never said it was that good. I wonder if he was gambling again. He said he wasn't gonna, but he was really into it. They say it's like drugs for some guys; they just can't stop. 'Course he coulda invented something; he was that smart. I bet that's what he did."

I was beginning to get the same lousy feeling I'd had with Jim Ralston. Brody wasn't a Mafia hit man or even a small-time hood. He was a decent guy who didn't have much going for him, and I'd just told him his idol was dead and that he was going to be rich. I was using him the way Sutton had used him and the way a lot of other people in his life probably used him. It didn't feel good. The damage was done, and there wasn't any way out, so I plunged on, wanting to get it over with as quickly as possible. The hole in his sweater was now the size of a silver dollar; I couldn't stand to look at it any more.

I asked a few more questions, then rose to go. "Thank you very much for your help, Mr. Brody. I'm terribly sorry to be the bearer of such sad tidings." It was time to cut and run, but I had one more thing I had to do. I stopped at the door, and put my hand on Brody's arm.

"I feel I should warn you of one thing before I go," I said, and this time the urgency in my tone was real. "There are problems with the will, and because of the issue of Mr. Stratton's identity, we can't be sure that the will we have is valid. Please don't spend any money or make any changes in your life until we contact you. I can't stress that enough. Several years ago, we were involved in a case where a man quit his job and put a down payment on a house only to discover a week later that his brother had made a second will leaving the money to someone else."

Brody looked confused. "You mean I might not get the money?" he asked.

"That's exactly what I mean!" I said. "Please don't do anything about it until you hear from me." I made a hasty retreat before he could ask any more.

Dinner at last, assuming there was still enough left of my stomach to accept it. I'd been running on adrenaline and nervous energy, but as I drove back across the Tobin Bridge, I became aware that my body was three hours behind my watch. Suddenly, the lobster dinner I'd been planning lost its appeal, and a bowl of clam chowder seemed all I could manage. I stopped at a small, cozy-looking restaurant with steamy windows and checkered curtains.

While I waited for my chowder, I looked over the print outs from the *Globe*. My guilt over Alexander Brody was replaced by elation as I read them. The robbery Brody described had to be the one covered in the July 16 edition of the *Globe*. Two thieves had been caught leaving the parking lot of Synitron, a large manufacturer of RAM chips for personal computers. The chips had been worth over a million dollars.

I remembered Jesse's lecture on the plastic cockroaches. The RAM chips he planned to buy cost about five dollars a piece. The ones stolen in 1978 had cost over a hundred dollars each. A real case of reverse inflation.

I read over the article again. One of the investigating officers was quoted in it. I circled his name in red. I could go down to the station and talk to him tomorrow. On the other hand, I could go home to San Francisco and call him on the phone. The phone won out over an extra day in Boston.

I caught the nine o'clock flight the next morning and was immediately aware that five hours of enforced idleness is cruel and unusual punishment.

I wondered what Peter had learned about Sutton and Monroe. So far all I had was supposition. The fact that Sutton had been involved in a major theft didn't make him a murderer, but it sure gave him a motive. It would also account for the professional thugs who'd helped frame Peter. They could easily have come from Sutton's former associates in Boston. I replayed the case in my mind several times. It always came out the same. Marilyn had discovered Sutton had access to the plans. She'd also either found out about his past or she'd gotten something else on him. She tried blackmail; he tried murder. A nasty little scene all round.

Even if I were right, knowing the killer's identity was only part of the job. We still had to prove it and prove it conclusively enough to clear Peter. I tried one plan after another, none of them worth the risk. Finally, I gave up; I'd have to hope my brain worked better on the ground.

Peter and Jesse were both out when I got to the office. No one had bothered to leave notes saying where they were going. I decided to take care of a loose end that had been bothering me. I suspected Marilyn Wyte had been blackmailing Sutton for the plans for the Alice chip design, and I also suspected that Sutton would steal them for himself if he could pull it off. But could he? Microcomp would certainly do everything in their power to keep the plans secret. I needed a bit more information before I could assess Sutton's chances of getting the plans.

I called Leo. "Who's got the best security system in the industry?" I asked.

Leo paused. "I'd guess it's I-Tech," he replied. "They had a big chip theft several years ago, and they really cracked down after that."

"Do you know anyone in security there?"

"No, but I imagine they'd be very helpful. Their chief of security is always trying to convince other companies to tighten up. He's something of a true believer."

I smiled. Leo did not like true believers, even when they agreed with him. I thanked him and was about to hang up when he exclaimed, "Wait. I almost forgot that I have a message for you. Miri wanted me to tell you that Susan Clayton will be at the Stanford Children's Hospital tomorrow from one to four. There's some sort of reception for new members of the Ladies Auxiliary, and she'll be one of the hostesses. Miri can introduce you to Susan if you'd like."

I'd have liked nothing better a few days ago. But now there didn't seem to be much reason for it. I thanked Leo and explained that I no longer had such a pressing need to meet Susan Clayton.

He seemed disappointed, and I sensed that Miri would also be disappointed. She'd probably gone to some work to set up a meeting. In the end I promised to try to get to the reception if my schedule allowed.

Leo was right about the chief of security at I-Tech. He was not only willing to help me; he was willing to see me that afternoon if I could get there by 4:15.

Peter and LeRoy sauntered in shortly before I was due to leave for Santa Clara. LeRoy was grinning like a kid with a secret he couldn't wait to tell, and Peter was obviously pleased about something.

Jesse met them in the front hall. "You see Mr. Monroe?" he asked.

"That we did," LeRoy announced. "The man was real helpful."

They trooped into my office with Jesse, Eileen and Amy following like Peter was the Pied Piper. LeRoy deposited his considerable bulk in a chair that was just barely strong enough to hold him, and Peter sat on the edge of my desk.

Everyone waited breathlessly. I thought they were laying it on a bit thick, but then maybe I was just jealous because no one ever got breathless about what I had to say.

"So?" I said.

"So, the good news is that our assumptions about Mr. Monroe were correct, he is indeed a spook; the bad news is that he is not our killer."

"You're sure?" I asked.

"Reasonably. He's certainly capable of ordering a hit, but from what we know, Marilyn's death was not in his best interest, and Mr. Monroe is a man who takes self-interest very seriously."

"Why was he seeing Marilyn Wyte?" I asked.

"She had something she wanted to sell, something of great value to a number of people."

"The plans for the chip design," I suggested.

"That's what she told him."

"He could have gotten the plans and killed her to keep her quiet or to avoid paying off."

Peter shook his head. "Monroe is a businessman. His business is selling secrets, and people like Marilyn Wyte are his suppliers. You kill off your suppliers, you have no product."

"What makes you so sure he told you the truth?" I asked.

"You'd seen him, you wouldn't doubt it," LeRoy put in smugly.

Jesse and Eileen were leaning forward so far that they were about to fall off the couch.

"You could say that I gave him very good reason not to disappoint me," Peter said.

LeRoy could contain himself no longer. "He slammed the dude up against the wall and explained how there were three ways you could break a nose so the doctors could never put it back together again. Then he described the different possibilities for broken jaws, shattered cheekbones. Sounded like a real leg-breaker. Man, I didn't know you knew all that shit."

"Only the stuff about noses. The rest I made up as I went along," Peter said mildly, obviously enjoying the rapt attention of the crew on the couch. "Monroe is a very vain man, cares a bit too much about his face. That can be a real handicap when you work outside the law."

He turned to me and read something less than whole-hearted enthusiasm in my frown.

"Hey, it sounds bad, but the violence was really minimal. I slammed him up against the wall, that's it. We got what we wanted with no broken bones on either side. And with a guy like Monroe, that's not bad."

I was angry, and I wasn't sure why, which made me even angrier. "Look, you had to do what you did, and you probably did it as well and with as little violence as possible, but you don't have to be so damn proud of yourselves for being meaner and nastier than the bad guys."

Peter looked surprised; in fact, everyone looked surprised. "Hey, lighten up, Catherine," he said. "There are some things you can't do by the book. Don't be so uptight."

That was it. Peter was sitting in my office playing Sam Spade for my staff and telling me not to be uptight. "*Up-tight* is how I got here, buddy," I snapped. "*Uptight* is what my clients like. The Bank of America is not *light*; it does not like *light*; it likes *uptight*." I turned to Jesse and Amy, "And in case you two have forgotten, its clients like the Bank of America who pay our salaries, not the Peter Harmans of the world."

I paused for breath and realized that they all looked confused and embarrassed. No one seemed to know quite how to react to my uncharacteristic outburst of emotion. It wouldn't have done any good to explain to them that I'd worked hard for the six years since Keith's death to build an agency that was respected for its discretion and reliability, and it had only taken Peter a few days to get everyone including me to start acting like a bunch of renegades.

I looked at my watch. Time to leave for I-Tech. "I don't have time to talk now," I announced. "My notes are on the desk, Peter."

14

I-Tech was just across the street from Microcomp. Its buildings were larger with no pseudo-Spanish pretensions, but its parking lot was smaller. After searching in vain for a parking place, I crossed the street and parked in Microcomp's visitor parking area.

Security at the front desk of I-Tech was considerably tighter than at Microcomp. The receptionist had my name, and a visitor's pass was waiting, but I wasn't allowed past the front desk without an escort. The receptionist dialed the Security department, and in a few moments a young man in a guard's uniform arrived to escort me to his superior.

Andrew Knight, Director of Security for I-Tech, was a professional. That was clear in the first few minutes of our meeting. He was in his fifties, had a medium build, graying hair, and a body that seemed twenty years younger than his face. Probably ran several miles a day. Something in his bearing told me he'd been in the military; army intelligence, maybe.

He welcomed me to his office; the decor was early corporate sterile with no personal artifacts to reveal that it was inhabited by a real human being. I seated myself in a modernish chair that felt better suited to inquisition than polite conversation. We chatted for a few minutes, establishing both of our credentials. Knight looked like the kind of man who didn't like to waste time, so I got down to business fast.

"I need to know some things about security in the computer industry," I informed him. "It's lousy," he replied. "Minimal at best, nonexistent most of the time."

"How is security at Microcomp?"

"The guys across the street? I don't know directly, but I can tell you that you can count on two hands the number of companies that have adequate security, and it's not one of them. Lot of these companies think security means hiring two guys in uniforms to stand around and ask people if they have a pass."

"So it might not be too difficult for an employee to steal from them," I prompted.

"Hell, it's not nearly hard enough to keep people from stealing from us; and I work full time at it," he said. "In the computer industry some of the most valuable parts are the smallest. Guy can slip a few microchips in his pocket and turn a handy profit. Hard to catch him and even harder to prove it."

"And trade secrets?" I asked.

"Harder still. And believe me there's plenty of buyers around. Guys arrive here with shopping lists. With thefts at least you have an object; with trade secrets, it can be just what's in a guy's head. Even the counterespionage people have trouble keeping a lid on."

"With something as complicated as the design of a chip, you'd need more than someone could carry in their head, wouldn't you?"

"Yeah, you'd need the plans, diagrams, probably formulas—lots more than anyone could remember."

"How do you protect plans and diagrams?" I asked.

"How do I protect them? Or how do the jokers with college degrees in public relations protect them?"

"If you were protecting diagrams, how would you do it?" I asked.

"Well, first if you're working with something you want kept secret, you set up a team at another location, get them out of the central office. Then you limit the number of sets of plans or schematics to two or maybe three, and those never leave the building. You set up a sign-out system so two guys have to sign for the plans when they take them out, and when they return them the plans go in the vault. You want two guys so that no one ever has them alone." He paused. "That's what I do."

"Sounds very effective. Where does it hang up?"

His eyes twinkled. He was secure enough in his competence to admit that even the best plans have a weak point. "It doesn't hang up if everyone follows directions, but, of course, they don't. The problem is that for a group of guys to work well together, there has to be respect and trust, so if your buddy carries a set of plans off by himself, you don't want to be a straight arrow and run to the supervisor. You give him the benefit of the doubt."

"So even with a good security system," I said, "a man could get the diagrams for long enough to photograph them."

Knight nodded. "Probably."

I felt a surge of excitement. If an employee could sneak photographs of diagrams from I-Tech, Tim Sutton could certainly get them from Microcomp. Things were finally coming together. I thanked Andrew Knight, and he escorted me back to the front desk.

I was hungry when I left I-Tech, and I certainly wasn't going to eat at Denny's again. If I took Highway 280 back to San Francisco, I could stop off in Portola Valley at a small inn that served marvelous French food. It was off the beaten track, but after all the miles I'd logged on the freeways lately, a drive through woods and pastures appealed to me.

The meal was far better than good, and the wine I drank with it combined with the effects of jet lag put me in a definitely rosy and not very alert mood. That's probably why it took me several miles to notice the white Porsche behind me. I damned myself for my carelessness. Now I was out on a country road with no one else around and someone on my tail.

I had a pretty good idea who the someone was. Tim Sutton drove a white Porsche, and he'd had just enough time to get the word from one of his buddies that I'd been asking questions. I didn't have to wait long to find out what he had in mind. The Porsche sped up and pulled out into the next lane to come alongside. He was either going to force me off the road, or he was going to try to shoot me. I didn't wait to see which.

I floored the gas pedal and blessed the friend of Dan's who'd talked us into putting a six cylinder engine in the Volvo.

The Porsche had plenty of power too, and my burst of speed kept it behind me but not by as much as I'd have liked. Sutton pulled back into the lane behind me, but the lights of his car grew brighter as he closed the distance between us.

The road took a curve to the left, and my wheels squealed as I forced the car through the turn. This was just the first of a number of turns, and they got sharper farther down the road. I doubted that I could make them at my current speed.

I wasn't going to outrun the Porsche, and going off the road was apt to be hard on both the Volvo and me. A long driveway loomed up to the right. I had no idea where it led, but I wrenched the wheel hard to the right and managed to skid into it. The Porsche followed.

I hoped that there was a house full of people at the other end of the driveway, but even if there wasn't, I preferred playing cat and mouse on foot to doing it in a car.

I rounded a turn and had to brake hard not to bump into one of several cars parked in front of a large farmhouse. The lower floor of the house glowed with lights, and I could see figures through the large windows on one side.

I was out of the car almost before it stopped, and I ran for the house in a stooped position that I hoped made me less of a target. I heard the Porsche squeal to a halt behind me, then roar into reverse. It was gone before I reached the door of the house.

I banged on the door, and it was opened by a tall woman in her early forties. She was wearing blue jeans, a Greenpeace sweatshirt and a very broad smile. She registered surprise as she realized that I wasn't whoever it was she was expecting, and the broad smile was replaced by a more sedate one. "Can I help you?" she asked.

I explained that someone in a white Porsche had tried to force me off the road, and she immediately ushered me into the house.

The room was casually furnished for comfort rather than style. A bright-colored Mexican rug covered the aging overstuffed couch, and none of the chairs matched each other or anything else in the room. The large old Oriental carpet on the floor might have been expensive but probably wasn't.

The two couples in the room were all in their early forties. The casualness of their appearance and attire suggested former hippies who were making only a modest effort to adapt to the upscale styles of the eighties. The faint odor of pot in the room confirmed my assessment.

An uncomfortable silence greeted my entrance. The tension gave way to expressions of concern when I explained my situation, and they realized I wasn't a narc.

"I guess we should call the police," the woman who had answered the door suggested, with a noticeable lack of enthusiasm.

I considered for a moment then shook my head. "No," I said. "I don't think that's really necessary." Everyone looked relieved but a bit puzzled.

I explained that I had a pretty good idea who was after me but no proof. "He's not dangerous to anyone else," I assured them, "and I don't want to spend hours at a police station filling out reports."

They looked grateful, and I suspect they believed I was just giving them a way out of a potentially difficult situation. In reality, my actions were motivated as much by self-interest as altruism. The last thing I wanted at this point was for Lou Martin to get involved in my investigation of Tim Sutton.

I wasn't about to head back out on the road where Sutton might be waiting for me. Time to call Peter.

"I just want to get home," I said, the weariness in my voice making the statement more plaintive than I'd intended. "Could I use your phone to call a friend in San Francisco to come escort me back."

A large man whose bushy hair was streaked with grey jumped up to offer his assistance. "Hey, no need for your friend to come all the way down here. We can get you back to the freeway, if you think you'll be safe from there."

Sutton would be no problem once I was on the freeway with plenty of other cars. He wouldn't risk anything where there were witnesses. I accepted the offer gratefully.

"It's the least we can do," the large man responded. "I think we should take you to the Bayshore; 280 doesn't have that many cars on it at night."

The second man offered to drive behind me. "You drive the pick-up and let me drive the wagon," he suggested to his companion. "Sorry, I won't have time to make the salad," he informed the woman who'd answered the door. He didn't sound sorry at all.

The drive home gave me plenty of time to think about Tim Sutton. Obviously, someone had tipped him that I was asking questions. It could have been the bartender at Spades,

Alexander Brody, or both. I wondered if he'd followed me from San Francisco.

The Buy America Brigade had certainly made me easy to spot, and I wasn't looking for a tail. But I'd been tired, not asleep, and I didn't like to think that an amateur could tail me that far without me noticing.

It was more likely that he'd spotted my car in the Microcomp parking lot. After all, a blue Volvo with *Buy USA* scrawled across it is a real eye-catcher.

To the best of my knowledge Sutton and I had never met, so I doubted that he'd recognized me. Alexander Brody hadn't seen my car, but someone else had—the bartender at Spades. I remember wondering why he followed me to the door. Was it to get a look at my car so he could describe it for Tim Sutton?

There was one spot of comfort in the night's adventures. Sutton had come after me alone. If the men who'd held Peter were still around, there would have been more than one car on that road.

Peter was waiting when I got home, and he wasn't thrilled to hear about the night's adventure. Dan had always become angry when he thought I was in danger. It was a pleasant surprise to find that Peter became tender. He wrapped his arms around me and held me for a long time, then said, "No more swipes at the blue bus."

"At least we can be pretty sure who the killer is," I said.

Peter nodded. "He's finally tipped his hand. Now there's just the little matter of proving it."

"I'm bushed," I admitted. "I'd rather tackle that one tomorrow."

Peter's arm was still around my waist. He drew me closer. "How bushed is bushed?" he asked.

"Not that bushed," I responded, snuggling into his arms.

Another Saturday morning, another meeting. With luck it might be the last one. Everyone showed up at 9:30, looking a bit groggy but not complaining. The story of what I'd learned in Boston and "the great car chase" woke them all up.

Sutton looked like the prime suspect, but I checked with everyone to make sure we weren't overlooking any other leads. Peter's visit to Spades revealed that gambling was probably as much a part of its business as selling drinks. The action was considerably heavier than a few friendly bets on the ponies. The fact that the bartender was the only one associated with Sutton who'd seen my car argued strongly for a connection between the two men.

Eileen's interviews with residents of the apartment house where Marilyn had lived in San Francisco had turned up a neighbor who'd known the dead woman. The neighbor was a very attractive Eurasian woman who worked for an escort service, and she'd confirmed what Marilyn's friend in Washington had suspected—that Marilyn had been working as a call girl.

Eileen had talked to the manager of the escort service that had employed Marilyn. "She quit when she moved to Palo Alto," Eileen announced. "The service had girls on the Peninsula, and they tried to convince her to keep working, but she refused. She was making a hundred dollars an hour not counting tips."

"Nice piece of change," Jesse commented. "And a nice piece of work. You ought to hire this lady, boss."

Eileen blushed at the compliment. I smiled at the thought of her interviewing Marilyn's beautiful neighbor and the manager of the escort service and wondered if she'd experienced the same mixture of embarrassment and fascination that I'd felt the first time I was in a similar situation.

Peter and Jesse bantered back and forth about the ethics of stealing promising employees until I pointed out that if we didn't get busy, I wouldn't have to steal Eileen because her boss would be in jail.

"Everything points to Sutton," Peter said. "Time to get some evidence we can take to the police."

"And how do you propose to do that?" I asked.

"We could take a look in his apartment, might be something there," Jesse suggested.

I gave him a thoroughly withering look. "Unless you have an invitation, that's breaking and entering."

Peter agreed. "The last thing we want is to get anywhere near Sutton's apartment. If there is evidence there, we don't want any possibility we planted it."

Jesse looked a bit chastened. "How do you feel about entrapment?" he asked.

"Better than breaking and entering," I said, realizing that Jesse's mind might be moving in a direction similar to my own. "What do you have in mind?"

"If he still has the plans, he's looking for a buyer. I could play the buyer, carry a tape and get him to incriminate himself."

We were on the same track, with one important difference. "I've been thinking along similar lines," I said, "except that I was planning to be the one with the tape."

Jesse looked disappointed, but not too disappointed. "You're the boss," he said.

"I'm also the one with the black belt, which gives me something of an advantage in this situation."

Amy chose that moment to come in with a tray of sweet rolls and a pot of fresh coffee. Peter was frowning, but he waited until the tray had been passed to speak.

"Even for a black belt, this could get dangerous. What if he's carrying a gun?"

"We'll set up the meeting for a public place, one where there are lots of witnesses and you guys can be fairly close without raising suspicions."

"He could try a drive-by hit."

"So we'll choose a place where that isn't possible."

"It's damn risky, and there's no guarantee you can get him to say anything incriminating," Peter objected. "He'd probably ID you and refuse to even talk. Then we'd only have succeeded in spooking him."

"He's already spooked enough to try to kill me," I pointed out. "I doubt that he has more than a general idea of what I look like. Last night he probably spotted me because of the car, but in case he can recognize me, I'll put a dark rinse on my hair and wear glasses. I'm fairly good at altering my appearance."

Peter looked skeptical. He tried a new tack. "What makes you think he hasn't already sold the plans to his old friends in Boston?" he asked.

"I expect he has," I replied. "They supplied the muscle, they certainly know about the goods. But I also expect that a man like Sutton won't be able to resist selling the same plans again if he thinks he can get away with it."

Peter considered. "He's a gambler. He might just be arrogant enough to try it." He wasn't convinced, but he was getting interested.

We kicked the plan around for a while. Peter raised every objection he could think of. He was right that it wasn't a great plan. I didn't even like it very much. I especially didn't like meeting a killer who might know more about me than we realized or who might recognize my voice. But it was the only plan we had, and in the end we decided to go ahead with it if we could find a meeting place that was safe.

We made the appallingly cliched choice of a public park. Sutton would be directed to sit on a bench that was visible from all sides and far enough from any noise sources so we'd get a good recording. I would join him on the bench. Peter would watch for accomplices, and Jesse would watch Sutton. It sounded like the script for a TV show. At least there you had the director on your side.

Eileen had been listening silently to our plans. Finally, she spoke. "I'd like to come, too."

Peter and Jesse looked dubious. Peter started to talk her out of it, but I interrupted. "If you think you can handle it, come along. We can use the extra help."

"I can handle it," she said, and the way she said it told me she could.

"All we need now is to find the park. Then we can make the call to Mr. Sutton," I announced.

* * * *

We took two cars and scouted out parks on the Peninsula. After comparing several that seemed possible, we
chose Rinconada Park on Middlefield and Embarcadero in
Palo Alto.

Rinconada had the advantage of being large but fairly
open. Even though the traffic was heavy on two of the streets
that bounded it, the center of the park was a good distance
from the streets. The playground equipment and other
spaces designed for children were at the western end of the
park, with tennis courts and a now-closed swimming pool
at the eastern end. We could arrange the meeting for the east
end, as far from the little kids as possible.

A small red building containing restrooms and an
empty snack bar sat a short distance from the pool and across
from the tennis courts. The bench in front of it was screened
from one street by the tennis courts and from the other by
the building. It was ideal for our purposes.

The tennis courts weren't close enough for their noise
to interfere with taping, but they provided a perfect cover
for Jesse. We could outfit him as a tennis player, and he
could appear to be waiting for his partner to arrive. If we set
up the meeting for today or tomorrow, the courts would be
full of potential witnesses, and Jesse would probably be only
one of several people waiting for a court.

We ran through the plan with Peter playing Sutton and
trying to figure out every possible way to kill me. Jesse and
Eileen tried different positions until they found spots from
which three people could defend against any scenario Peter
and I could come up with. It was a little eerie to plot my own
murder, but I'd never given an assignment more attention.

"I think we want to set the meeting as close to the phone call as possible," Peter suggested.

I agreed. Once I'd contacted Sutton, I didn't want to give him time to arrange an ambush or to get cold feet. It was 2:30 now, and it'd take about two hours to dye my hair and transform myself into someone else. I had what I needed with me; Peter had his gun. We could be ready for a meeting by 5:00.

"I think we're ready now," I said. I looked around the group. "Any reason we shouldn't go ahead and do this as soon as possible?"

No one came up with one. I turned to Eileen. "Are you sure you want to go through with this?" I knew she could do it, but I wanted to make sure she knew it.

"I can handle it," she said calmly.

She sounded a lot more confident than she probably felt inside, but looking the part is a good first step, and I was glad for her.

We drove to Eileen's apartment in Palo Alto to call Tim Sutton. I hooked the tape recorder to the phone. The tape wouldn't be admissible in court, but it might contain something of interest to the police.

Sutton picked up the phone on the third ring.

"Is this Tim?" I asked.

"Yes, who is this?"

"I'm a friend of Marilyn's," I said. "I work for some people who are real interested in something you have."

"I don't know what you're talking about," Sutton responded. His voice was tense.

"I think you do. I sure hope so, because I have a business proposition for you."

"I don't know what you're talking about," he repeated, less adamantly this time. "But if you want to offer me a business deal, I'll listen to you."

"Good," I said. "The people I work with would like to purchase the merchandise you discussed with Marilyn. They're prepared to offer a very good price. If you'd like to discuss it, we could arrange a meeting."

There was a long pause, then Sutton responded. "All right. I'll meet with you." He paused again.

Before he could suggest a time or place, I said, "Fine. Meet me at 5:00 at Rinconada Park in Palo Alto."

Sutton seemed taken aback. "No, no, I can't meet tonight," he stammered. "It'll have to be tomorrow."

"Tomorrow will be all right," I replied. "One o'clock in the afternoon. I'll call you at noon to tell you where to meet. And, Tim, I don't know what happened between you and Marilyn, but I work for a large organization, and my associates would take it very badly if anything were to happen to me. You understand?"

"I don't know what you're talking about, but if you want to talk business, I'll be there at one." He hung up.

He hadn't whimpered, whined, and blurted out a full confession, but then I really hadn't expected him to. Sure would have been nice though.

I looked at my watch. It was 2:45. I really didn't have any excuse not to drop by the Stanford Children's Hospital and see Susan Clayton.

15

I pulled into the Stanford Children's Hospital parking
lot and deposited Peter's scruffy old MG between two sleek
silver BMWs. It looked like I felt—overworked and under-
dressed. At least I hadn't worn jeans.

I spotted Miri over by the registration desk, talking with
a younger woman who'd just stepped out of a *New Yorker*
ad. They were a study in contrasts. Miri was short and wiry,
her curly dark hair flecked with white, a tiny package of
dynamic energy. Her companion was stately testimony to
what good bone structure and money can do for a woman.
She carried just the right amount of weight on about five feet
seven inches of graceful height, and topped it off with wavy
blond hair. If she turned out to be Susan Clayton, Peter
would have some explaining to do about the obvious omis-
sions in his description of her.

Instead of interrupting their conversation, I stood a short distance away where Miri could see me. After a few moments, she directed the woman to someone at a desk on the other side of the lobby and came over to join me. I thanked her for her help and tried to reassure her that the case was going well without telling her how well. She led me to the inner courtyard, where Susan Clayton was chatting with prospective volunteers.

Susan was several inches shorter than the woman I'd seen with Miri, but she had the same classic good looks. Her blond hair hung straight to the shoulder then flipped under. She wore a blue dress with a beige linen jacket. Her Italian leather heels matched the blue of her dress exactly and probably cost more than my entire outfit.

"Tell her I asked to meet her because I thought we'd gone to school together," I suggested. "That way you'll be off the hook." Miri nodded, led me over to Susan, and introduced me as I'd suggested. Before we could begin talking, Miri excused herself to get back to the lobby.

There wasn't much point in beating around the bush. "I lied to Miri," I announced. "We've never met, but we have a friend in common, and I need to talk to you."

She looked surprised but unruffled, not quite the pose she'd presented to Peter.

"My friend is Peter Harman," I announced. That got a reaction. She was visibly shaken; she recovered quickly, but tension hardened her previously gracious exterior.

"What do you want?" she asked in a low, strained voice.

"Just to talk," I replied. "Is there some place less public around here?"

She led me back into the hospital and down the hall to a small lounge with coffee and snack machines. The room was empty. I had a sudden desire for coffee even if it came from a machine, and I suspected Susan Clayton could use something to get through the next few minutes. "Coffee?" I asked.

She nodded absently. I wasn't even sure she'd heard me, but I got two cups anyway.

We sat at a small round table in the corner. "I need to know why you hired Peter," I said.

"For the reason I told him, to get evidence that would help me get custody of my kids." She was studying the cup as though she could read some answer there if she just looked hard enough.

"Infidelity doesn't affect custody decisions. Peter must have told you that," I said.

"He did."

"So why did you hire him to follow your husband?"

"I was desperate." She said it in a deadened voice that sounded depressed rather than desperate.

"I believe that, but I also know from Peter that you're too bright a woman to bet on a sure loss."

She hesitated. She'd finished her coffee, and now she began dismantling the Styrofoam cup, tearing away a piece of the rim, then another piece. I watched the tiny pieces of Styrofoam drop from her fingers to form a half circle around the cup.

"It was a long shot," she said, "but I hoped the pictures of at least one woman would show bruises or something."

I waited as she continued to dismember the cup and worked up the courage to tell me what she couldn't tell Peter.

"I was hoping Peter would find evidence that he'd beaten one of them. I can't prove he beats me, but if I could prove he beat someone else maybe someone would listen to me."

"So he does beat you," I said.

"Oh yes. Not too often and rarely so it shows, but he slaps me around."

"You could go to the police. The fact that he batters you would be grounds for both divorce and custody."

She shook her head. "His doctor would testify that I did it to myself. I have a history of depression. They could make me look crazy and take the kids. He mustn't get the children," she declared with a startling ferocity. "Jennifer's at the rebellious stage. He slaps me around because I don't keep her in line. If I weren't there, he'd beat her. I can't let that happen."

The stakes were higher than I'd guessed, and I knew at once that there was no chance Susan Clayton would testify for Peter or that we could ask her to.

I arrived home to find Peter, Jesse, and Eileen giggling around a game of Trivial Pursuit.

"Thank goodness you're here," Peter boomed. "These poor youngsters don't have a chance against an old pro."

I studied the board. "How come Jesse has all the pies?" I asked.

"Because he cheats," Peter exclaimed. Jesse was about to protest when Peter stopped him with a stern, "No one could get that many absolutely easy questions without cheating or divine intervention."

I started to suggest that there must be a better use of our time than Trivial Pursuit when I realized that of course that was exactly what we all needed. We'd gone over the next day's meeting several times more than necessary. Rehashing the plan would only make us tense when we needed to be calm. "There's beer in the fridge and pizza on the way," Peter announced.

"You'd better not have drunk all the Weinhard's," I warned, heading for the kitchen. Peter had once made the mistake of finishing off my Henry Weinhard's and replacing it with some American beer with a German name and absolutely no flavor. He was great with wines, but he'd drink just about any beer as long as it was cold.

The fridge had enough beer to suggest that Peter was planning on a long evening. At least it was the right brand. I pulled out a bottle of Weinhard's and headed back to the living room. "Somehow I'd hoped for something more than pizza as my last meal," I said.

"I should hope so," Peter responded. "But this is not your last meal; it may not even be your last meal for the evening."

Jesse stifled a snicker. He knew better than to laugh out loud since he was as avid a late-night snacker as I was. Between the two of us, we knew just about every place you could get something decent to eat after midnight and before dawn. It was one of the hazards of the profession.

I hadn't even started drinking, and I felt light-headed. A quick count of empty beer bottles revealed that there weren't nearly enough of them to account for the general level of hilarity. A little alcohol and a lot of tension can be a heady combination.

The doorbell rang, and I went to answer it, figuring it was the pizza and hoping Peter hadn't ordered anchovies. It was Dan.

"Dan, come in," I said, feeling vaguely awkward.

"Jesse ordered the anchovies," Peter called from the other room, followed by raucous laughter.

Dan ignored the crew in the living room. "I have some news that may be relevant to your case," he said.

"Come on in." I ushered him into the living room. Peter and Jesse were noisily disputing whether Peter's answer to a Sports and Leisure question was too vague. They fell silent immediately. Then both rose to greet Dan.

"Hello, Harman," Dan offered, extending his hand.

Peter shook hands, and introduced Eileen and Jesse. The formalities over, they stood awkwardly eyeing each other.

"Dan has some information about the case," I explained. I motioned Dan to a chair, acutely aware that Peter occupied his favorite place at the end of the couch.

"One of the names you asked me to check was Tim Sutton, wasn't it?" Dan asked.

Peter and I exchanged glances. "Yes," I answered tensely.

"We got a report that a man by that name was killed in a car wreck on Skyline Drive a couple of hours ago."

"Was he driving a white Porsche?" I asked hoarsely.

Dan nodded.

Eileen let out a little gasp but except for that, the room was very silent. Peter slumped back on the sofa and stared blankly at the ceiling. Jesse studied the floor. I felt as if someone had just hit me in the stomach.

My eyes took in the room, but my mind was blank. When it began functioning again, I realized that Dan was waiting for someone to explain the dramatic impact of his announcement. "Sutton killed Marilyn Wyte," I explained. "We would have had proof tomorrow."

Dan understood at once. "And now?" he asked.

I shook my head. "Nothing."

He nodded, and his usual neutrality was replaced by an expression of genuine concern. "I'm sorry," he said. There wasn't anything more to say. With his usual sense of tact and timing, he rose to go. He put his hand on Peter's shoulder, "If I can help, Harman, let me know."

At the door, he paused. "You should call Lou Martin and let him know Sutton is connected to the Wyte case. There may be evidence in his apartment."

"I'll do that," I said. "Do you have any details on the wreck?"

"No, but if you'd like, I'll see what I can get."

"I'd appreciate it," I replied. "I'm particularly anxious to know if there's anything that suggests foul play."

"I'll check," he promised. "But in a bad wreck it's usually damn near impossible to tell."

I'd guessed as much. As I walked Dan to the door, I was struck by the eerie realization that in the story I had fabricated for Sutton's friend, I had predicted the exact form of his death.

Peter was sitting just as I'd left him. Jesse and Eileen were conversing in low tones. There wasn't anything we could do tonight, so I sent them home and promised to call in the morning.

I got the brandy from the dining room and poured Peter a generous glass. He drank it down like water, not even wincing. He sat in silence for a few moments more then drew me close for a hug. "Damn rotten luck," he said.

"If it is luck," I countered.

"You mean maybe it wasn't an accident," Peter suggested. "How much of that is wishful thinking?"

"Some. But remember, Sutton couldn't meet this evening. Maybe he had other plans. Maybe he was meeting someone else." Peter considered it.

"Maybe," he said.

The doorbell rang. I went to claim the pizza that no one wanted. As I carried it to the kitchen, I overheard Peter on the phone.

"LeRoy, it's Peter. I need some help. Is Carlos still in the same business? Good. I may need to take an extended vacation abroad. Can you find out where he'd suggest I go and what he'll need to arrange things?"

There was a pause. Peter's back was to me so I couldn't see his expression, but his voice was grave. "Yeah, it is bad. Listen, tell him right-wing dictatorships are out. I'll call you tomorrow night. And thanks."

He turned to face me and must have read the dismay in my face. He took me in his arms. "I'm not skipping out just yet," he said. "But the way things are going, I'd be a fool not to take some precautions. If it comes to that, Catherine, I am not spending my life in jail."

He was right, of course; and my initial shock was just the vestiges of my policeman's daughter upbringing. But what really bothered me was something else, something I couldn't bring up. Where did I figure in his plan? Was I to take him to the airport and kiss him good-bye before he flew off into the sunset, or was he assuming I'd come along?

I wanted him to care enough about me to ask me to come with him, but I didn't know what I'd say if he did. I couldn't handle the idea of marriage, and now I might very well have to choose between Peter and my life in San Francisco. That was as scary as facing Marilyn Wyte's killer.

We talked about the case for a bit, but we were both wrapped up in our own thoughts, and I felt increasingly lonely and isolated. Finally, Peter announced that he needed to be alone for a while and said good night.

I went to bed depressed and woke up depressed. Since it was a Sunday and I couldn't think of a single thing to do, I grumped around the house for most of the morning. By afternoon I was disgusted with myself and decided to go out for a walk. It should have cheered me up, but it didn't. Every time I tried to think about the case, I felt like my head was full of mashed potatoes.

It took me a good part of the day, but I finally realized that what I needed was to go to the dojo and work out. Aikido was the surest way of getting on top of the wave of messy emotions that continued to assail me. The 4:00 class on Sunday was a general workout, open to students of all levels. I could make it if I hurried.

I felt the calming effect of the dojo as soon as I walked in. It was comforting just to stand in the large light-filled room. I checked in at the office and explained that I'd need someone else to take my classes next week. Any other time, Frank would have given me a bad time for skipping so many classes, but today he simply nodded sympathetically and told me to take the time I needed. I realized I must look really awful to command such instant sympathy.

The workout confirmed my appraisal. I rolled like a box, and my timing was off. But as so often happens during a workout, my mind quieted and another kind of awareness took over. I began to sense and respond to the energy of my partners, and movement became a form of meditation. By the end of class I felt lighter and quieter than I had all week.

As I drove home, I could finally think clearly about my situation with Peter. It had taken me almost twenty-four hours to remember the lessons I tried to teach the beginners. You can only respond to what's there, not what might be there. It was useless to worry about whether or not Peter wanted me with him. I could only wait until he'd made the decision for himself. Then I could confront the question of whether or not I'd go. In the meantime, while I was waiting for my life to sort itself out, there were things I could do—like work on the Marilyn Wyte murder and Tim Sutton's untimely death. And now that I'd dumped some of the clutter out of my mind, perhaps I could get on with that.

Monday morning was foggy in the city but clear and beautiful in Palo Alto. I was at the Palo Alto Police Department at 9:00; Lou Martin walked in at 9:10. "I have some information for you," I said as I fell into step with him.

"Come on in," he offered in a tone that was a long way from enthusiastic. He stopped to pour us both coffee that had probably been brewed the day before and escorted me to his office.

I told him about Tim Sutton's relationship with Marilyn Wyte, what I'd learned about Sutton's past, and my theory about the theft of the chip design process. I also told him of Sutton's death. He listened impassively, nodded a couple of times to reassure me that he hadn't gone to sleep, and jotted down some notes on a stray sheet of paper. When I finished he asked, "You going to give me the name of the alleged spy and the other guy she tried to blackmail?"

"No," I replied, "not at this time. If we get to the point where that information will help clear Peter, I'll give it to you."

He'd known that would be my answer, but he didn't look pleased. He doodled for a minute then announced, "We'll check Sutton's apartment." He opened a desk drawer and searched for a file. "I got the bank records you were interested in," he announced.

He found the file and surveyed its contents without showing them to me. "In addition to her monthly salary Ms. Wyte received a sizable monthly payment from a dummy corporation we have as yet been unable to trace." He paused to let the information sink in. "Interesting, isn't it?"

"A dummy corporation?" I repeated. He nodded. "And just one check per month." It sure wasn't what I'd expected, but it had to mean something. "What do you make of it?" I asked.

"I was about ask you that," Martin responded.

"Sounds like either blackmail or a salary," I replied. "Were all the checks for the same amount?"

"Just about. The amount increased twice but then remained steady at the higher amount."

"It almost has to be blackmail," I suggested, "but with just one victim."

"The one is pretty hefty," Martin announced. "We're checking the source of the checks, but whoever set up the dummy corporation did a good job of hiding his tracks."

I'd dealt with that sort of thing often enough to know what he meant and not to expect success soon.

"How long has she been getting these checks?" I asked.

"We only asked for the last year's records. She received them throughout the entire year."

"She moved down here from San Francisco two and a half years ago. I'd be interested to know when the payments began."

"I would, too. I should have that information this afternoon. I might be willing to share it, if you wanted to tell me why you're interested in it."

That stopped me. If the checks went back the full two and a half years, then Clayton was pretty certainly their source. But I had no proof of that, and giving Martin his name might reveal Susan's role in the case. My dad taught me to always tell the truth; Peter's policy was to tell the truth when you couldn't come up with anything better. In this case they both came down to the same thing. "I want to help you, but I have a problem," I explained. "If the checks go back two-and-a-half years, I have a pretty good idea of who wrote them. But there's an innocent person mixed up in this, and I have to find a way to protect that person's identity."

"Your decision," Martin said. "You decide to cooperate, call me for the information."

I needed to think through the implications of those checks, and I wasn't about to share my half-formed thoughts with Lou Martin, so I thanked him and made my exit.

One check, one source—if it was blackmail, it sure wasn't the type we'd expected. Marilyn had dated a lot of different men, but only one paid her, and that one had been paying for at least a year. The only one we knew for sure she'd seen steadily for that long was Hugh Clayton. He was a likely source. Yet I just couldn't see him as a blackmail victim.

If Clayton was the source of the checks, he was also a prime suspect in the murder. But if Sutton wasn't the killer, why had he tried to force me off the road Friday night? There were too many loose ends, too many things that didn't fit.

Then there was the possibility of a wild card. What if it wasn't Clayton? If it wasn't any of the men we knew about? It could be someone from Marilyn's past, someone she'd known in San Francisco. Two days ago, I would have been appalled by the idea of starting over; today I'd be grateful for anything that didn't point to Tim Sutton.

I called Peter, but he wasn't home and he hadn't come into the office.

I spent the trip home mulling over what I'd learned, but I hadn't found any answers by the time I got to the office. It was almost as if I had two separate cases that had to meet somewhere but didn't. The checks argued for blackmail and a killer who got tired of paying. But the timing suggested that Marilyn's death was tied up with the plans for the new design process. I pulled out my notes and went over them again. Somewhere there was a connection I'd missed, a question I should have asked.

Three times through, and I still didn't see it. I felt myself beginning to tense up, to try to force an answer from the pages. Aikido had taught me that never worked. There's a time for focused concentration, and there's a time to relax and listen to a different voice. I'd done the first. It was time for the second.

16

I went for a long walk, sat in the park and looked at the view, and finally went home. I wasn't any closer to the answer, but I felt better.

I was in the shower when it came to me. It had been there since my conversation with Martin that morning. When he'd asked my reaction to the checks, I'd responded that they must be either blackmail or a salary. Two possibilities, and I'd chosen the wrong one. I'd spent so long thinking of Marilyn as a blackmailer that I hadn't even considered the second possibility.

The checks weren't payoffs; they were payment. And Marilyn wasn't the blackmailer, she was working for someone else. That someone had to be Hugh Clayton. Clayton, the man who could turn information into money, or find a place to sell stolen parts. It was an elegant scam. A beautiful woman who didn't appear too bright but was an appreciative and admiring listener could get many men to tell her almost anything. A little wine, a romantic interlude, and if all else failed, the threat of blackmail. All Clayton had to do was aim her at the right man and wait for her reports.

But apparently Clayton had gotten more than he'd bargained for. Marilyn was ambitious, and when she got her hands on the plans for the Alice chip design, she decided to free-lance. That, of course, was why he killed her. He'd framed Peter to provide the police with an open-and-shut case and prevent too thorough an investigation of Marilyn's affairs.

I rinsed the shampoo from my hair and jumped out of the shower. As I was drying off, I remembered something else that suddenly took on new meaning. Marilyn Wyte was not the only woman Hugh Clayton was seeing. There had been several others. They were probably in the same business as Marilyn.

The other women were the key to the case. If I could get one of them to confess to the police, I could establish both that Clayton was involved in industrial espionage and that he had an excellent motive for murder. What would it take to get one to talk? The threat of a murder charge combined with a promise of immunity ought to do it. Marilyn wasn't a hardened criminal, just an opportunist who hadn't many scruples. If the others were like her, it wouldn't take much to convince them to save themselves and throw their boss to the wolves.

I called Peter. Still no answer, and no message with my answering service. I called the office. It was after five, and Eileen was the only one still there. I asked her to wait while I threw on some clothes and headed for the office.

* * * *

I went over my theory with Eileen. It felt right; everything fit. There still wasn't enough to bring the police in; we needed a confession from one of the women. Getting confessions was one of my specialties. I suspected that Clayton's girls would be easier to deal with than corporate crooks.

Eileen found Peter's notebook with the addresses of the women he'd followed. There were four besides Marilyn. The closest was Sally Trilson. She lived in Daly City, just south of San Francisco, about thirty minutes away. I could be there by a little after six, which would probably be about the time she got home from work. I copied her address on a three-by-five card and told Eileen what I was about to do.

It was a sign of how far she'd come that she didn't fuss over me or fret that it was too dangerous. She listened carefully, then said, "Wouldn't it be better tomorrow, with Peter and Jesse to back you up?"

It would, of course. But I wasn't sure we had that much time. Clayton's next move might be to go after Peter or to move his girls so we couldn't find them. In either case, we couldn't afford to wait.

It was Monday; Jesse would be at his computer group. I figured I could handle Sally Trilson myself, but being of a cautious nature, I wasn't heading off without some form of backup. "Can you wait here to handle the phone?" I asked Eileen.

"Sure."

"Good, I'll call you around seven o'clock to check in. No, I might need longer, make that seven-thirty. If I don't call, it means something's gone wrong." I gave her Dan's number and told her to call him and explain where I'd gone and why. Being saved by my macho ex-husband was not a pleasant prospect, but it was better than the alternative.

I stopped at home to change out of my jeans. The impression I made on Sally Trilson would have a big effect on how cooperative she was. I was going for intimidation. I wanted her to feel like she was having a cozy chat with her local district attorney. I put on my charcoal business suit and low-heeled shoes.

I also took my black leather attache case. Ruffling through papers while shaking your head and frowning unnerves the toughest customers. I learned that one from the tax auditors.

It was the tail end of rush hour, and I arrived at Sally Trilson's apartment complex right on schedule. Like Marilyn Wyte, Sally lived considerably better than your average secretary. Her apartment was in a set of two-story wooden buildings tastefully arranged around internal courtyards. The courtyards were planted with a profusion of attractive trees and shrubs that provided the illusion of privacy and intimacy despite the large number of people housed there.

I parked in front of the complex and went looking for apartment 117. I found it on the ground floor of one of the buildings on a courtyard toward the back. I rang the bell. No answer. I rang again and waited. I hoped I wouldn't end up sitting in my car, waiting for her to come home. More than that, I hoped she hadn't gotten scared and run.

Finally, I heard footsteps and the door opened, but not much more than a crack. A dark-haired young woman in her late twenties peered out at me.

Something was clearly wrong. She didn't look exactly scared, but her caution was unnatural. "I'm Catherine Sayler," I began. Before I could continue, the door swung open, revealing a large man standing next to the girl. He was holding a gun, and it was pointed at me.

"Come right in, Miss Sayler," he said. He pushed the girl to the side and stepped back to make room for me. I considered running; he probably wouldn't shoot me down in the courtyard, but "probably" just didn't seem good enough balanced against the gun. I stepped into the apartment.

He motioned me over against a wall, and closed the door; then he spoke to the girl. "Go on, Sally, get your stuff. You don't need to concern yourself with Miss Sayler."

Now that I could see the girl, I could tell that she was frightened. I didn't know whether it was me or the man with the gun that made her that way. She looked from him to me, then said in a pleading voice, "Brennan, please—"

"It's okay," he cut her off. "Just get your stuff like I told you. The boss'll take care of things."

She retreated to the next room, and Brennan turned his attention back to me.

I realized with some surprise that I wasn't frightened. All the training in the dojo was paying off. I watched Brennan and waited. It wasn't so different from waiting for an opponent to strike. I didn't think he was going to shoot me, not right now anyway, so all I could do was wait.

My stillness seemed to bother him. Finally, he said, "Take your jacket off, real slow. Drop it on the floor."

I took it off and dropped it on the floor.

"Now, turn around and put your hands on the wall."

He was going to search me, not a pleasant prospect, but possibly an opportunity. If I was lucky, he'd put his gun away while he did it. I turned and moved close to the wall so I'd be balanced if I had a chance to strike. Brennan didn't move toward me. "Move your feet back," he ordered.

I pretended not to understand.

"Move your goddamn feet back," he snarled. He moved to the side and kicked me hard in the shin. I let out a howl, and moved my feet back.

"Farther," he growled, and I did as he said, ending up in such an impossible position that if I tried to take my hands off the wall I'd fall on my face.

He put his gun back in the holster, but that wasn't going to do me any good in the position I was in. He took his time searching and was a good deal more thorough than he needed to be. Feeling his hands on my body and myself helpless to do anything about it, I struggled against rage, then fear.

When he was finished, he ordered me to sit down on the floor next to the wall. Sally Trilson came back into the room carrying a small suitcase and looking as uncomfortable as I felt. Brennan had her sit in a chair.

"Where's the phone?" Brennan asked her.

"On the little table, next to the door to the kitchen," Sally answered in a small voice.

He went over to the table without taking his eyes off me. I tried to see the number he dialed, but couldn't. It probably didn't matter anyway. I was pretty sure who "the boss" was, and I had a feeling I'd be seeing him soon enough. Brennan identified himself and reported that he was at Sally Trilson's apartment. "Guess who showed up," he announced with what seemed like pleasure. "Catherine Sayler. Yeah, that's right. Find out what the boss wants me to do with her."

There was a pause just short of forever, and Brennan grunted, "Yeah, sure," and hung up.

He slouched back to the sofa and sat down, keeping the gun neatly leveled at my head.

Waiting for a few minutes is one thing, but waiting longer gets harder. Too much time to think. Brennan looked like he was settling in for a long wait; I was going to get a real chance to practice all I'd learned in the dojo about staying centered. I tried repeating to myself the old rule: *Pay attention to what is, not to what might be; stay in the moment.*

Sally wasn't having any easier time waiting than I was. She fidgeted and wiggled, finally trying to engage Brennan in conversation.

"Where do you want me to go? I could just go to the airport and take a flight somewhere myself. Maybe that'd be better. It'd be less trouble for everyone."

Brennan shook his head. "The boss'll take care of everything. Just do like he says, and stop worrying."

If his words were vaguely reassuring, his tone was not. I wouldn't have given much for Sally's chances with "the boss"; I doubted that the plans he had for her involved an airplane trip. She could have been an ally. But scared as she was, she wasn't ready to act. She still harbored some hope that she'd be all right, and she'd probably keep right on hoping until Brennan turned his gun on her. But then she hadn't read the autopsy report on Marilyn Wyte.

I couldn't even estimate how long we waited. It seemed forever. Then there was a knock at the door, and Brennan sent Sally to answer it. A large, burly man with thinning sandy hair came in. I knew him at once from the sketches Peter's artist had produced.

He glanced around the room, and his eyes lit on me. "Nice work," he complimented Brennan. "The boss is real pleased. You want me to tie her hands?"

"Naw," said Brennan. "Just make us look suspicious." He motioned for me to get to my feet. "Fold your arms in front of you," he ordered. I did as I was told.

Brennan picked up my attache case and stuck my purse inside it. He carried the case and had me walk in front of him. The sandy-haired man walked with Sally. They led the way to a dark blue sedan in the parking lot.

Brennan opened the back door, and motioned me in. I started to unfold my arms as I climbed into the car, but froze when he barked out, "Watch the hands." I wondered if Brennan knew about my black belt, or if he was just cautious. Whatever the reason, he wasn't fooling around.

Everyone waited while I climbed into the back seat. Brennan followed me in and told Sally to sit in front with the driver. I glanced over at Brennan. A silver digital watch on his wrist displayed the time—7:19. It would be eleven minutes before Eileen would even consider calling Dan, probably longer. If he acted immediately and made all the right assumptions, it would still take him at least an hour to check Sally Trilson's apartment and drive to Clayton's house. I doubted that I had that long.

17

If I'd had any doubts about the identity of Marilyn Wyte's killer, they disappeared as the car took the offramp for Woodside. The driver turned up the driveway to Clayton's house and stopped at the gate. A man emerged from the bushes, looked into the car, nodded, and let us through. Somehow I wasn't getting much pleasure out of having my suspicions confirmed.

The house was large and expensive, but I wasn't paying much attention to architecture. I was too busy checking out the windows and doors. The driver got out and opened my door; Brennan shoved me out so I landed on my knee, looking up into the barrel of the driver's gun. Peter was right, these guys were pros. They hadn't made a single careless move, and it didn't look like they were going to.

Before I'd regained my feet, Brennan grabbed my wrists and twisted my arms behind my back. I don't know if there's a painless way to do that maneuver, but he clearly wasn't looking for it.

He shoved me onto a path that led around the side of the house and up to a double glass door at one end. The doors led into a study, and just inside the door stood Hugh Clayton. "Good evening, Catherine," he greeted me congenially. Absolutely cool; he could have been ushering me in for dinner. It sent an unpleasant sensation up my spine.

Clayton stepped to the side so I could see the figures behind him. There were two men and Peter. Peter was standing funny; then I realized that he wasn't standing as much as being held up by the man behind him. He looked up at me with a pained expression; the skin under his right eye was beginning to swell and darken with a bruise. Brennan shoved me over to Peter's side.

"Mr. Harman and I have been discussing a business deal. Unfortunately, he has been rather uncommunicative. I hope your presence will encourage him to be more cooperative."

"Let's try it again, Harman. I want to know why you were following Marilyn Wyte and who paid you to do it."

"Answer hasn't changed, Clayton." Peter said hoarsely.

One of the men moved in to hit Peter again, but Clayton motioned him back. "Get smart, Harman. I want that information, and I am prepared to do whatever's necessary to get it. I'm not going to play games. You know I'll have to kill you both. If you tell me what I want to know, you'll die quickly and painlessly. If you force me to get that information the hard way, things will get very unpleasant. Markham here"—he motioned toward the man who'd started to hit

Peter—"is extremely skillful at persuading people to do what he wants them to. I think he rather enjoys it."

So do you, you bastard, I thought. I moved my arm slightly and Brennan's grip tightened. Not good.

Clayton walked to his desk and pulled something out of the drawer, then recrossed the room. He stopped in front of me and opened his hand slightly as the blade of a knife flicked open. My stomach felt like someone had just dropped a rock in it.

He moved the blade slowly to my shoulder and placed it against the flesh just below the bone. Then very deliberately he drew it across the skin leaving a three-inch long slash. I fought back the urge to struggle and scream and managed just to wince and catch my breath, but Clayton wasn't watching me. His eyes were on Peter's face. He smiled.

"Markham, I think we'll concentrate on Ms. Sayler." He looked back at me with the same ugly smile. "You really should have stayed out of this, Catherine; as I told you at dinner, it's not a good business for a woman." Then he turned to Peter. "It's all up to you, Harman. Say the word and Markham will stop. We have all the time in the world, but I hope for Ms. Sayler's sake that you decide to cooperate soon."

Since there wasn't really much else I could do, I decided it was time for some hysterics. Whatever chance we had, and at the moment it didn't seem like much, lay in convincing these men that I was weak and utterly helpless.

My lip quivered. I burst into sobs. "Peter," I wailed, "don't let them hurt me. Peter, please." It was a lousy thing to do to Peter. He'd know it was an act; I'd practiced my "hysterical woman" routine in front of him to get it right. He knew what I was up to, but I could still see that my cries and entreaties stung him. He clenched his teeth and turned his head away.

"Peter," I shrieked desperately, then dissolved into sobs.

Clayton nodded toward the door and Brennan pushed me toward it. "Don't take too long, Mr. Harman," he cautioned.

"No," I shrieked loudly several times. There's nothing like a woman's screams to unnerve some men. I hoped it might have that effect on one of our captors. But Clayton stepped forward and slapped me hard across the mouth.

"None of that," he snapped. "You can scream all you want in the wine cellar, but if you do it again up here, I'll gag you."

So much for screaming. I gulped, hung my head and sobbed softly.

Markham and Brennan took us out of the house again and across to a small outbuilding beyond the pool. Markham opened the door, and Brennan pushed me ahead of him down a short flight of stairs. At the bottom, I decided that it was time to act. I faked a stumble, which pulled Brennan off balance, and in the moment that his attention was diverted I pulled my hands loose. He reached for me, but this time I was ready. The move went as smoothly as if we'd been working out in the dojo. I spun him out around me and then snapped him in close to my body with his arm twisted at an angle that would discourage any effort to move. We froze there in a brutal embrace. Brennan tried to move once, moaned in pain, and gave up the effort.

Markham pulled his gun and jammed the muzzle against Peter's head. "Let him go, or Harman dies," he growled. Here was a man who watched too much TV.

"No, Markham" I said. "We're already as good as dead. You'll have to do better than that."

Markham paused. I didn't waste time wondering what he'd do next; I was busy trying to remember exactly where Brennan kept his gun. I searched for the image, the moment he slid it back into his holster—a shoulder holster—left side.

Markham suddenly shoved Peter towards me, sending him crashing against Brennan. In the moment that Peter's body came between us, I reached for Brennan's gun, stepped to the side and fired.

Markham looked mildly surprised as the bullet knocked him backwards against the wall. He started to raise his gun, and I fired again. This time the gun dropped, and Markham's body slumped to the floor. I was fairly sure he was dead.

Beside me, Brennan was trying to get to his feet. I brought the gun down heavily on the back of his skull, and he collapsed.

"Not bad for a woman who hates violence," Peter commented, as I struggled to untie the rope on his wrists.

"Any idea of how to get out of here?" I asked.

" 'Fraid not."

"Can you walk?"

Peter nodded. He took the gun from Markham's hand. "Let's go back toward the main gate."

We retraced our steps up the stairs. The wine cellar must have been soundproof since there was no sign that anyone had heard the shots. Peter and I slipped into the bushes and began working our way back to the main gate. Fortunately, much of the driveway was lined with oleander bushes.

We were nearing the gate when all hell broke loose back at the house. We started to run. No need for subtlety now.

The oleanders formed a thick hedge near the gate, but beyond them lay open fields with no place to hide. We crouched behind the bushes as two cars raced to the main gate and braked to a stop thirty yards from us. A shot rang out, and I threw myself to the ground.

I hate being shot at. I didn't like the other things that had happened that evening either, but I have a special horror of being shot by someone I can't see and don't even know is there until the bullet hits me.

"Watch for the flash of the gun and shoot at that spot," Peter instructed me.

I forced myself to raise my head enough to watch for the flash. A bullet crashed through the branches above my head. I didn't see where it came from because my face was buried in the dirt.

"Watch for the flash," Peter repeated.

Again I forced myself to look up. My hand was shaking in a decidedly unheroic manner. I hoped Peter couldn't see it. Time to put all that training from the dojo to work. I concentrated on my breathing and tried to clear my mind. Just as I was beginning to get control, another gun barked, and a bullet crashed through the bushes nearby. This time I saw the flash. It came from behind one of the cars. Not much chance I'd ever hit someone with that kind of cover. Peter fired back. He didn't hit anyone either.

I was waiting for my life to flash before my eyes and wishing I'd paid more attention to Dan's marksmanship lessons, when I heard the siren. At first, I dismissed it as a traffic bust, but the sound continued to come closer. Finally, there was no doubt that the squad car was headed our way.

"It's the cavalry," I whispered, being careful to keep my head down.

"Yeah," said Peter. "Give me your gun."

"Why?"

"Just give it to me for a minute."

I handed it over, and as he carefully wiped the handle on his shirt tail, the awful truth hit me. "The cavalry is bringing the rope," I observed.

"They're not coming to congratulate us on cracking the case. I am the prime suspect in a homicide, you are my girl-friend, and we are on the estate of a wealthy and influential businessman whose bodyguard has just been shot with this gun. Which do you think they're going to believe— kidnapping or breaking and entering?"

"And you're going to take the rap for the murder."

"For the moment. We can't do much to prove our innocence from the inside of a jail cell, and you'll have a lot better chance of getting out on bail if you're not charged with murder."

I had to admit that he was right though I didn't like the idea of him taking the rap for me.

The cruiser pulled up next to the other two cars and stopped. I strained to see who was getting out of it. There were two men, one in uniform and one in a suit. I couldn't be sure, but the stocky figure wearing a suit could be Martin. I stood up and raised my hands well above my head and walked toward the group of men. Peter was just behind me. "Lieutenant Martin," I called. "It's Catherine Sayler. Peter Harman is behind me."

The stocky man shined his flashlight directly in our faces, blinding me so that I could no longer see him. When he spoke, it was indeed Lou Martin. "Harman, you know this violates the provisions of bail. You're under arrest." The uniform stepped forward to take charge of Peter.

"Miss Sayler, I wouldn't have thought you'd get mixed up in clearly illegal activity. I guess I misjudged you." His voice was hard, and his hand was unpleasantly firm as he took hold of my arm just above the elbow and propelled me toward the police car. "Put your hands on the car, please."

It took me a moment to realize that he was about to frisk me for a gun. I forced myself to put my hands on the police car. Martin's search was strangely tentative and carefully chaste, a pleasant contrast to my experience earlier in the evening. It wasn't until he began to read me my rights that it finally got through to me that I was being arrested.

I wasn't looking forward to going through booking and spending the night in jail, but it was a definite improvement over the previous possibilities.

Martin shined his light on my arm. It looked even worse than it felt. "What happened to you?" he asked.

"Ask the man at the house," I replied.

He peeled the fabric from around the wound. "It's stopped bleeding," he said. He took out a handkerchief and carefully wiped away the worst of the blood, then fumbled in the glove compartment and came up with an elastoplast to put over it. "That'll take care of it until we get to the station," he said.

A second cruiser arrived, and Martin ordered the officers to take statements from Clayton's thugs. He pulled out a pair of handcuffs, and announced almost apologetically, "Knowing your background in martial arts, it would be imprudent not to use restraints."

The feeling of the cold metal on my wrists brought home as nothing else had the fact that I was now defined as a criminal. After all that had happened that night, being arrested should have been a relief, but I felt my eyes sting and had to fight back tears.

Martin took my arm again and shoved me into the back seat of his cruiser next to Peter, announcing that we were going up to the house to get a statement from Clayton.

Once in the car he turned to me. "Dan Walker called me. I would like to believe that my instincts aren't so wrong that I've let you make a fool of me. Before we get to the house, is there anything I should look for that might support the possibility that you didn't break in here?"

"Look for a young woman, Sally Trilson. She was brought here with us. She worked for Clayton, but she wasn't involved in the murder. She's probably very frightened. Clayton's men talked freely enough in front of her that I don't think they were planning on leaving her alive." I stammered out what seemed to be our last hope. Unless Martin could find the girl and convince her to talk, even he couldn't get us off the hook. I prayed that this wasn't going to be a replay of the Tim Sutton situation.

Clayton was standing in the doorway as we drove up to the house. I shuddered as I recognized his silhouette and realized to my dismay that the emotions I'd worked so hard to control were dangerously close to the surface. I concentrated on my breathing.

Clayton greeted Martin with a story of how his bodyguard had surprised us breaking into his study and captured us. Clayton had ordered the bodyguard to take us to the wine cellar until the police could be summoned. Michael Markham, a security officer from Clayton's company, had offered to go along and help out. When they hadn't come back, Clayton had gone to investigate and found the bodyguard unconscious and Markham shot to death.

Where he'd been the cool businessman when I last saw him, he was now the distraught employer. His performance was flawless. I wondered if Martin would even bother to go through with the search.

My heart sank when he began to console and reassure Clayton. Then to my relief he explained gently that he wanted to search the entire premises to make sure that there were no accomplices still hiding on the property.

Clayton seemed taken aback. He assured Martin that he and his employees had searched the house and the area around it and found no one. Martin was apologetic but insistent. "I hate to put you and your family through this," he explained, "but this is a murder case."

Two more police cars pulled up, as if to emphasize the seriousness of the situation. Martin instructed the officers to search the house and outbuildings and bring anyone they found to the living room. He opened the door of the cruiser and ordered Peter and me to get out. We were escorted to the living room.

* * * *

The search took long enough for me to begin to realize just how bad the situation was. If Martin didn't find Sally Trilson, the search would be a routine part of a murder investigation in a case that could only be described as open and shut. I tried not to speculate on what kind of sentence we'd get or what jail would be like. I glanced at Peter. The bruise under his eye was a deep purple and his lower lip was cut and swollen; he was watching Clayton, who stood across the room giving a statement to one of the officers.

In the bright light of the living room I got a better look at myself. It's amazing how much blood a superficial wound can produce. My sleeve was soaked with it, and the front of my blouse and skirt were covered with large dark stains. The cut wasn't nearly as bad as it looked, but it was probably the end of my sleeveless blouse days.

The maid was escorted into the room; then a couple of men I didn't recognize were brought in. Susan Clayton did not appear to be home. Finally, Martin returned. Sally Trilson was not with him.

"That's about it," he exclaimed.

"Did you search the wine cellar?" I asked desperately. He nodded. "What about the pool house? the basement?"

"What is this?" Clayton interrupted. "What kind of an investigation is this where the criminal asks the questions? Those two killed my friend. I want them out of my house." The emotion in his voice gave me hope that he had something to fear from a search; I struggled to think where Sally might be hidden. Martin nodded to the officer standing behind us, and took my arm and pulled me to my feet. "Let's go," he said.

As we reached the door I remembered Clayton telling me about riding at dawn. If there were horses on his property, there must be a stable. "The stable," I gasped.

"Stable?" Martin asked. "Do you have a stable, Mr. Clayton?"

Clayton exploded. "I've had enough of this," he bellowed. "These people break into my house and kill one of my employees, and you question me like I was the criminal." Martin ignored him. "Mueller, Jacobs, find the stable and check it," he ordered.

Clayton ordered Martin out of his house and began hurling names of community leaders who wouldn't like the way he was being treated. Martin made some conciliatory comments, but if Clayton's thinly veiled threats bothered him, he gave no sign of it.

After what seemed an endless wait, Mueller and Jacobs returned, bringing with them a very frightened Sally Trilson. Before anyone could speak, Clayton burst out, "My God, there was another one of them."

At the sight of Clayton, Sally burst into tears and clung to the officer who had brought her from the stable. The other policeman explained, "We found this woman in the stable, sir. She was tied up and gagged."

Before Clayton could speak, Martin announced, "I think we'd better sort this out downtown. I'm afraid I'll have to ask you to come with us, Mr. Clayton."

Martin had Sally escorted to his car and sent Peter and me in one of the other cruisers. Clayton asked to drive his own car, but Martin insisted on his accepting the "hospitality of the department."

If Martin believed our story, he hadn't let the other officers in on it, and the two men in charge of Peter and me clearly believed that they were bringing in Bonnie and Clyde. We were still a long way from being home free. If Sally told the truth about this evening's events, we wouldn't be charged with Markham's death, but we hadn't cleared Peter of Marilyn Wyte's killing.

Even with that unpleasant awareness, the back of the police cruiser felt deliciously safe, and I began to relax for the first time that night, only to discover that relaxation was a mixed blessing. My shoulder started to throb, my neck hurt when I moved my head, and the inside of my mouth ached.

I looked over at Peter and realized that he must be even more uncomfortable that I was. He turned and asked, "How are you doing?"

"My shoulder hurts and the inside of my mouth feels like raw hamburger."

"I'm sorry" Peter said, and there was something in his voice I hadn't heard before. "I'm sorry about what happened, and I'm sorry about what could have happened."

I realized that while the relative safety of the police car had allowed me to become aware of my physical injuries, it was having a different effect on Peter. The pain he was feeling didn't come from the beating he'd taken.

"Hey," I said, "that's the first time a client's been sorry I saved his neck."

Peter laughed hoarsely. It was a long way from his usual hearty laugh, but it was about as good as you could expect from a man in his situation.

We rode on in silence, listening to the crackle of the police radio. It reminded me of the rare occasions in my childhood when my dad had allowed me to ride in a squad car. I didn't want to think about how he'd feel about my current situation.

The look on Peter's face suggested that he was probably running through some of the awful things that might have happened at Clayton's that evening. I made a stab at distracting conversation.

"I got to Clayton's through a combination of brilliant insight, carelessness, and bad luck." I announced. "How did you get there?"

"With less insight and more carelessness," Peter snorted. "Since we were back at square one, I went back to where I started—the two men who grabbed me. I sent their pictures to Boston, then checked out the only other place they could have come from—Clayton's. I staked out his factory, and around four o'clock Brennan came ambling out with some other guys.

"Unfortunately, while I was watching Brennan, someone else was watching me.

"Clayton figured I was working for someone who wanted to cut in on his business. He was just tickled pink by the opportunity to get that information out of me."

We were nearing the police station. Peter said, "You should probably have an attorney before you say anything."

I'd given the matter a good deal of thought during the ride. If ever there was a situation where it was prudent to have your lawyer present, this was it. But protecting ourselves on this charge could well cost Peter his only chance to prove himself innocent of Marilyn Wyte's murder. If Clayton walked out of the police station, the first thing he'd do would be to destroy any evidence linking him to the crime. Martin had to break the case tonight, and the only way he could do that was with our help. "I think it's time to be completely honest with Martin," I said.

"That puts you in considerable jeopardy," Peter pointed out.

"Less than you're in if we don't talk. I'm planning on telling the police about tonight, everything, exactly as it happened, including the shooting," I said.

He smiled. "Figured you would," he said. "At least we won't have to worry about getting our stories to match."

18

We didn't come in through the front door of the police station this time. They brought us in down below, in the garage with the barred door that goes up when the squad car enters and comes down before you get out of the car. The cops loaded their guns, clubs, and mace into a locked compartment before they took us out of the car. They weren't taking any chances.

They led us to a room with two metal benches at opposite ends and handcuffed us each to a bench. The officer in charge of me looked about eighteen years old. He announced very stiffly that they would need to take a blood sample, fingerprints, and photographs.

"Are you booking me?" I asked.

"Not at this time, unless we are forced to by your refusal of the procedures I've just outlined," he responded, sounding like he was reading from the manual.

I agreed to the procedures.

When they had my fingerprints, blood samples, and what had to be the worst photograph I'd ever had taken, they repeated the process with Peter, then led us up a set of metal stairs to the main floor.

I'd known Dan would be at the station, but it was still a shock to see him leaning on the sergeant's desk. If I harbored any illusions about my appearance, they were at once dispelled by the shock and concern I saw in his face. I couldn't tell if his reaction was caused by how bad I looked or the handcuffs on my wrists.

Dan's eyes shifted to Peter and the look he gave him would have "frosted the devil," as my mother used to say. Then Dan's face hardened into professional neutrality, and he walked over to me.

"I think I'd better get you a lawyer, Catherine," he said. "Don't say anything until he gets here."

I almost laughed at the spectacle of Peter wanting to tell all and Dan urging the protection of a lawyer, but it only underscored the seriousness of the situation.

I thanked Dan but shook my head. "No lawyer," I said. Before I could say more, the officer at my side moved me forward. He didn't like Dan's interference any more than Dan would have in his place.

Dan stopped him. "That woman needs medical attention."

The cop looked at my arm and seemed to realize for the first time that the blood was mine, not someone else's. "We'll see she gets it," he promised.

They took Peter down the hall and led me to an interrogation room. The walls were a washed-out pink color that reminded me of medicine my mother used to give me as a kid. I read someplace that pink was supposed have a soothing effect. It didn't work for me.

True to his word, the patrolman called for someone to look at my arm. A uniformed cop with a medical kit responded. He peeled off the elastoplast, took out a brown bottle and some sterile cotton, and proceeded to clean the wound. It hurt like hell, and he made no attempt to be gentle, a clear case of police brutality. He bandaged my shoulder, snapped his bag shut and left—all without a word.

I'd hoped to see Lou Martin, but instead a cocky young detective bustled in. He was all officious importance, and his goal was to intimidate me. However, after an evening with Hugh Clayton, I was not impressed. He was so concerned with his own performance that he failed to notice that I was ready to make a full statement, and we played twenty questions until my irritation got the best of me.

The third time he asked about my relationship with Peter Harman, I exploded.

"Dammit," I said, "I have been kidnapped, slapped around, threatened, and shot at. I have killed a man, and all you can think to ask about is my sex life."

That stopped him short. "What man?" he asked.

"One of Clayton's hired thugs," I replied. "Would you like to hear about it?"

Once I'd gotten his attention he was a fairly decent listener. He grabbed a tape recorder, and I gave him my version of the night's events. Martin came in towards the middle and leaned against the wall listening. I repeated for him my theory about the connection between Clayton and Marilyn Wyte. The young detective wasn't in the least interested in the Wyte case; he only wanted to know about Markham, and to my annoyance, Martin made no effort to shift the focus of the inquiry. We went over the scene at Clayton's house several times, and it became clear that no one believed I had shot Markham. They assumed I was covering for Peter.

After the fourth or fifth time I'd described exactly how the shooting occurred, Martin took the detective outside to confer. A few minutes later he came back alone.

"Right now I'm not too concerned about which of you shot Mr. Markham," he announced. "Either he was a hood, and it was self-defense; or he wasn't, and I'll hang you both." He paused to make sure I'd gotten it. There was no question but that he meant exactly what he said.

He went on. "I want to know about Hugh Clayton's possible role in this. I think it's time for you to tell me what you know, all of it. Let's start with what sent you to Sally Trilson's apartment."

"You did," I replied. "When you told me about Marilyn's mysterious checks." I told him everything I knew about the case and everything I suspected, everything except Susan Clayton's involvement.

He noticed the omission. "And the reason Harman was following Clayton in the first place?"

"That involves the person I need to protect," I said. "I can only tell you that it is not in any way related to Clayton's criminal activity or the murder."

I expected him to press on that one, but he didn't. To my surprise, he smiled. "Not bad," he said. "Damned good, in fact. It matches what the Trilson girl gave us."

Someone knocked on the door and Martin went out to speak with him. He was back a moment later, smiling. I hoped the smile was a good sign. "You're right about the setup," he informed me. "He recruited call girls, put them through a secretarial course, and placed them where he wanted them. Trilson's worked for him for over five years.

"Blackmail was actually a small part of the operation; a lot of the information was freebies, just guys shooting off their mouths. If that didn't work, the girls suggested that they had a friend who paid for information. Trilson figures she's recruited a bunch of guys who still work for Clayton; they let him know when they come across something he might want."

"Do you have enough to hold him?" I asked.

"Oh, yes, there's kidnapping and blackmail for starters, and I expect we'll have more by the time we talk to all the girls."

"But not murder," I said.

"Not the Wyte murder, but probably Tim Sutton's. The search of Clayton's house turned up what appears to be the plans Sutton stole from Microcomp and a box of stuff that probably came from his apartment. The maid's given a statement placing a man matching Sutton's description at Clayton's house last night and leaving with Brennan and Markham around ten o'clock."

"So Sutton did have an appointment with Clayton," I said. "He must have been trying to sell Clayton the plans."

"That's my guess. We can't prove it conclusively without a confession, but I'm convinced Clayton had him killed. The autopsy report on Sutton says he died from a blow to the head. My guess is that the blow came before the accident.

They killed him, stuck him in his car and pushed it off a mountain. I'll have a fingerprint crew go over the car tomorrow."

"When Sutton tried to force me off the road, I assumed he was the killer," I explained. "Now I'm less sure of his motive."

"I think you can assume he didn't mean you well," Martin replied. "He wasn't a killer, but he was a thief, and he had plenty of reason to want you out of the way."

I nodded. "Do you have anything on the Wyte murder?" I asked.

"Not yet," he answered. "The Trilson girl can't help us there. However, I plan to spend a lot of time with Mr. Brennan, and I think we can convince him not to take the fall for Clayton."

"Where does that leave Peter?" I asked.

"Trilson's testimony clears you both of tonight's mayhem. Markham's death is a clear case of self-defense, so it doesn't really matter who pulled the trigger. While we don't have enough proof to charge Clayton and Brennan in the Wyte case, there's enough to make it damn hard to try Harman. I'd say he's home free on that one, too."

A sense of relief flooded over me, followed rapidly by a sense of exhaustion. I'd been holding it together, but now that we were really safe and I didn't have to tough it out with the police anymore, I was on the verge of tears. I bit my lip and looked down at the table to avoid Martin's eyes.

He paused to allow me to collect myself, then asked gently, "Are you willing to repeat everything you've told me in a sworn statement?"

"Sure," I responded. The tears had passed. I was ready to get this thing over with.

I gave my statement then waited in the interrogation room while someone transcribed it. I was beginning to doze off when Martin came back. "There's someone in my office to see you," he announced.

"Someone" had to be Dan Walker. Just what I needed at this point. Being treated like a felon was better than the disapproval or the sympathy I could expect from my ex-husband. But I owed him, and the least I could do was be gracious in my thanks.

Dan looked like he'd had almost as hard a night as I had. His usual immaculate grooming was shot. There were dark circles under his eyes, and his cheeks were covered with stubble. I felt an immediate surge of sympathy for him.

He stepped forward and folded me into his arms. It felt good—safe and comforting. I pulled away gently after a moment. "You saved my life," I said. " 'Thank you' seems a bit inadequate."

"Thank God we were in time," he exclaimed. He looked at me with an intensity that was unnerving. The old warning bells sounded in my head.

The long night was finally getting to me; standing up took too much energy, but I didn't want Dan to see that. I perched on the edge of Martin's desk.

I was grateful to discover that I wasn't going to be subjected to a lecture on my carelessness or a catalog of the horrors that might have befallen me, but the silence was becoming awkward. Dan's reference to being in time reminded me of something that had been bothering me. "I spent the ride to Woodside trying to figure out how long I'd have to hold out for you to reach me, but Martin was there a lot sooner than I'd hoped for. When did Eileen call you?"

"Just after seven, I think," Dan replied.

I laughed. "Thank goodness Eileen confused the time. I told her seven-thirty."

"It was too damn close as it was," Dan declared. "I drove to Daly City, found your car in front, the apartment empty, and your jacket on the floor. I knew how much you paid for that jacket, there was no way you'd leave it lying on the floor."

We both laughed at the thought.

"Come on, I'll take you home," he said.

I stiffened. Tired as I was, I hadn't seen that one coming. "I'm sorry, I'm waiting for Peter."

Dan exploded, "Damn it, Catherine, Harman almost got you killed tonight." He regained control quickly and said no more, but he couldn't hide the anger and hurt.

I realized with a shock that he had expected my brush with death to convince me of the error of my ways. And since he saw Peter as the cause of the whole thing, he assumed I'd reject the man who nearly got me killed in favor of the one who'd rescued me.

In the past I would have railed at him for assuming that Peter had gotten me into something when I managed to blunder in on my own. I was too tired tonight. It just didn't seem that important anymore. "I really do appreciate what you did tonight, but it doesn't change things," I said. I kissed him softly on the cheek and stepped back. Dan nodded and managed a smile.

Lou Martin was standing in the hall grinning like a matchmaker, but he lost his smile when he saw Dan's face.

They exchanged pleasantries, and Dan headed for the parking lot. Martin looked at me and shook his head. "I'll never understand women," he said.

I had a long wait while they transcribed my statement, plenty of time to think. I'd killed a man. The idea of it bothered me, but the fact of shooting Markham didn't. If I'd known him for more than a couple of ugly hours, I might have felt some loss at his death. There were no doubt reasons he'd become who he was and a time when he was something else. But in the end he'd chosen to be a killer, and I wasn't going to beat myself up because I hadn't chosen to be his victim.

Something else was bothering me. My mother's voice kept whispering, "Men don't like women who do too well; they want to feel that a woman depends on them." I'd rebelled against her advice, but it had cost me several relationships and a marriage. I'd outdone myself tonight— solved the case and saved our lives; I wondered if I'd also lost my man.

Eventually, the statement came, and I signed it. Martin walked me to the lobby. "Harman'll be along soon," he announced.

The sky outside was just beginning to lighten. It had been a long night. My shoulder ached, and my mouth was sore. I had a dull headache and a strong desire to sleep. I was considering the problem of how we were going to get home when they brought Peter out.

He looked awful. He had trouble standing straight, and he walked funny. One eye was swollen shut, and his lip was split.

"You're a mess," I said fondly.

"Matches the way I feel," he replied. The damage to his mouth made his speech slightly slurred. "Martin says you turned down a ride home with a real prince to wait for me. He was obviously not impressed by your judgment."

"That's me, faithful as a hound," I joked. "I'm hard to get rid of."

"I'm glad," he said, and put his arm around me. I started to give him a hug, but he winced and I drew back. I sensed something more than sore ribs separated us.

"Let's get out of here," he said. "I've spent too much time in this place."

We walked outside. The air was chilly and clean, refreshing after the stale air of the interrogation room. The sky was a deep blue. Peter took several deep breaths. "I feel like shit," he announced.

"You need some sleep," I suggested.

"No, I mean I feel like shit about last night. I screwed up, and damn near got you killed."

"We both screwed up enough to let Clayton get his hands on us," I pointed out. "You're probably feeling bad because you didn't break the ropes on your wrists, take the guns away from those two thugs, and carry me to safety on a white horse. That's reasonable."

He laughed in spite of himself, though it obviously hurt. "Yeah, I guess that's the way I feel," he admitted.

"Well, I can overlook it if you can," I offered.

He put his hand on the back of my neck and slid his fingers up through the hair, then drew me very gently against him. "You're sensational," he said. "And you were incredible with those two thugs, absolutely incredible."

He started to kiss me, and we both pulled back in pain. "You can't hug, and I can't kiss," I joked, "We're going to have a great love life for the next week or so."

"No need to rush," Peter replied, "We've got plenty of time."